A MONSTER ATE MY PACKED LUNCH!

PAMELA BUTCHART

nosy crow

Look out for:

BABY ALIENS GOT MY TEACHER!

THE SPY WHO LOVED SCHOOL DINNERS

MY HEADTEACHER IS A VAMPIRE RAT!

ATTACK OF THE DEMON DINNER LADIES

TO WEE OR NOT TO WEE!

THERE'S A WEREWOLF IN MY TENT!

THE PHANTOM LOLLIPOP MAN!

THERE'S A YETI IN THE PLAYGROUND!

ICARUS WAS RIDICULOUS

THE BROKEN LEG OF DOOM

First published in the UK in 2021 by Nosy Crow Ltd
The Crow's Nest, 14 Baden Place,
Crosby Row, London, SE1 1YW

Nosy Crow and associated logos are trademarks and/or registered
trademarks of Nosy Crow Ltd.

ISBN: 978 1 78800 969 0

A CIP catalogue record for this book will be available from the British Library.

Printed and bound in Great Britain by Clays Ltd, Elcograf S.p.A.

Papers used by Nosy Crow are made from wood grown in sustainable forests.

MIX
Paper from
responsible sources
FSC® C018072
www.fsc.org

3 5 7 9 10 8 6 4

www.nosycrow.com

Contents

The SURPRISE Trip

When we found out that our class was going on a school trip to a LAKE, we were SHOCKED. Because last time we went on a school trip, Miss Jones said, "NEVER AGAIN!" when we got back. And then she'd run off the bus and hugged her partner for

ages.

That's when Jodi (my best friend) said that it was SUSPICIOUS that we were ALL OF A SUDDEN allowed to go on a school trip again and that she had a WEIRD FEELING about the LAKE and that lakes were a bit

CREEPY.

Zach said that we were just OVERREACTING because that's what he ALWAYS says at first when STUFF happens to us. But then we find out that our

2

teachers are VAMPIRE RATS or that there are PHANTOM LOLLIPOP MEN floating around the school or that the SHEPHERD'S PIE is POISON and he changes his mind.

Maisie keeps saying that we should all apply to go to a NEW SCHOOL where the dinner ladies aren't DEMONS. But, like Jodi says, who would save our school if WE weren't around?

But when we got to the LAKE, Jodi didn't look so sure about saving anyone THIS time. And that was probably because of the WEIRD SIGN and the BANSHEES and the big muddy FOOTPRINTS.

But it was when we found Gary Petrie's ROBE down by the water that we KNEW.

There was a

MONSTER
IN
THE
LAKE

and it was coming to get us!

"WE'RE ON OUR OWN!"

When we got off the bus we were all SHOCKED. And it was obvious that the teachers were shocked too because their mouths were all hanging WIDE OPEN.

That's when Miss Jones made us all get back on the bus and said that we must have come to the wrong place. And we knew that she'd said it because this place looked

MEGA FANCY

and it even had two FLAGS outside the reception and bushes cut into SHAPES.

Then, just as Miss Jones was about to get back on the bus with us, a woman came rushing over with a HUGE smile on her face and she yelled, "Welcome! Welcome!

Welcome to our Luxury Lakeside Retreat and Spa!"

So that's when Miss Jones told the lady that there must be some sort of mistake and that we were on a SCHOOL TRIP and that she had booked an adventure week at MENTORS LAKE.

That's when the woman got a bit of a weird look on her face and she said, "Oh yes. That's us! You booked with us before we changed our name and added our luxury spa! But we still cater for school trips, don't worry. We LOVE children here!"

Then the woman clicked her fingers and

an old man appeared and started taking our bags out of the bus while she rushed us all inside the hotel reception.

Then the old man reappeared with a tray with fancy glasses on it and said, "Champagne?"

So we all looked at the teachers and saw that they were smiling

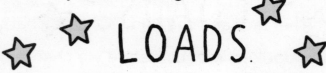 LOADS.

And then Miss Jones said, "No thank you. Oh well. Maybe just a tiny sip."

Then Gary Petrie told the old man that he went to places like this ALL THE TIME

with his mum and that he'd like a sip too. But the old man just laughed and walked away.

And that's when Gary shook his head sadly and said, "Ah well. No tip for him then!" And then he took a wallet out of his pocket and showed us and we saw that he had

LOADS

of money in it!

So I said that we were only allowed to bring **TWENTY POUNDS** with us because that was what the letter home had said. But then Gary said that it **WAS** twenty pounds and that he had just got it changed into old **ONE-POUND NOTES.**

That's when the woman came over to us with a bunch of keys and said, "Tam will take you to your luxury lakeside lodges now. Supper will be served in the hotel at 8pm."

The teachers looked

SHOCKED

again and Miss Jones asked about the **LUXURY LAKESIDE LODGES** and the lady said that we'd been **UPGRADED**

and that the lodges had HOT TUBS and BUTLER SERVICE.

And that's when Miss Jones

GASPED

and the other teachers started smiling loads and whispering to each other and Mr Beattie clapped his hands and said, "WOO-HOO!"

So we all followed Tam down to the lakeside lodges and when we got there he said, "They're all yours. Enjoy!"

And that's when the teachers went WILD and started running in and out of the

different lodges and shouting things like, "OH MY GOODNESS!" and "THIS ONE'S MINE!" and "THERE'S A POOL TABLE IN HERE!"

Then Miss Jones and Mr Beattie started ARGUING about which lodge they wanted and we just had to stand there for AGES until Gary Petrie eventually stepped forward and suggested they do ROCK PAPER SCISSORS.

I didn't think that the teachers would do ROCK PAPER SCISSORS but then all of a sudden Miss Jones got a REALLY SERIOUS LOOK on her face and put her hand behind her back and said, "One. Two. Three. GO!"

And then she shoved her hand out in front of Mr Beattie's face and we saw that she had made her fingers do SCISSORS. But then we saw that Mr Beattie's hand had done a ROCK, and rock BEATS scissors.

Mr Beattie yelled, "YES!" and said that he wanted the

GIANT

lodge with the POOL TABLE. And then we all had to watch as the boys marched

inside and Gary Petrie even stood and did a SALUTE at us before slamming the door shut behind him.

But then Miss Jones said, "Don't worry. We might not have the big lodge but there are THREE lodges left for us and they're all wonderful!"

So we all RAN into the first lodge and I

wanted to stay because it looked AMAZING
and it had one of those MASSIVE sofas
shaped like a CAPITAL "L", but Jodi shook
her head and said, "Follow me."

And she ran past the second lodge (even
though it was the biggest out of the three!)
and into the smallest lodge and yelled,

"THIS IS OURS.

Come on!"

And I was actually a bit ANNOYED at Jodi
because we hadn't even got to LOOK at the
other lodges properly and she was deciding

that we were getting the WORST LODGE.

But then when we got inside I saw why Jodi had wanted the SMALL lodge and it was because it was actually RIGHT in the lake and had a WHOLE WALL OF GLASS so it felt like we were actually in a house on the WATER.

I gasped and stared at Jodi and said, "How did you know?"

And Jodi smiled and said that she'd asked Tam on the way down which was the best lodge so that she could be PREPARED and make sure we were the FIRST ONES IN. And that Tam had said this one because of

the lake and the WALL.

And then she said, "AND ... it only has one bedroom so we all get to sleep together with

NO TEACHERS!"

And that's when Maisie gasped and said, "Wait. You mean ... we're on our OWN?!"

Jodi smiled and nodded and said, "We're on our own!"

ROBES!

As soon as we were unpacked, we had to go to the **MEETING POINT** for the **FIRST ACTIVITY** and we knew that because back at school Miss Jones had given us an

ACTIVITY ITINERARY.

DAY 1
ARRIVE. GET SETTLED IN.
FIRST ACTIVITY: NATURE WALK.

DAY 2
AM: RAFT BUILDING.
PM: ROPES COURSE.

DAY 3
AM: CRATE-CLIMBING.
PM: THE BIG JUMP!

DAY 4
AM: TUG OF WAR.
PM: OBSTACLES AHOY!

DAY 5
HOME.

Jodi was MEGA EXCITED and she was
wearing her new EXTREME SPORTS
OUTFIT that her mum had got off the
internet and it could read her BODY
TEMPERATURE and had a built-in
SWIMMING COSTUME and TORCH. And

she said that she'd used all her BIRTHDAY MONEY to get it in case we were made to do

SURVIVAL TRAINING

or

EXTREME

MOUNTAIN CLIMBING

and maybe even

WHITE-WATER RAFTING

and that she wanted to be PREPARED.

That's when I started worrying that maybe I should go back to the lodge for my waterproof jacket because I only had my shorts on and my new Sponge Bob T-shirt from Asda. But then Gary Petrie turned up wearing a white DRESSING GOWN and SLIPPERS and I stopped worrying.

Miss Jones rolled her eyes when she saw Gary and told him to go back to his lodge and get changed out of his dressing gown

RIGHT AWAY.

But Gary said that it WASN'T a dressing gown and that it was a ROBE. And that it had been left in the lodge by the HOTEL and that he was obviously MEANT to wear it. And then he started going ON and ON

about how when he was at a luxury hotel in MEXICO for his mum's wedding he'd had a ROBE and SLIPPERS there too and that he knew what he was doing.

But before Miss Jones could say anything else, the old man called Tam appeared again and said that he was a RANGER and that we could call him RANGER TAM. And that our first activity was a NATURE WALK and that Miss Jones was welcome to come or she could join the other teachers for TEA AND SCONES in the hotel. And that's when Miss Jones forgot all about Gary wearing the ROBE and rushed off.

Jodi nudged me and GROANED and said that she didn't want to go on a nature walk and that she wanted to do something EXCITING.

But then Ranger Tam overheard us and he said, "I think this nature walk might surprise you, lass. It's getting dark. And there's a LOT of creatures that only come out at night. Let's go."

So we all followed Ranger Tam into the woods.

And that's when Maisie started to SHAKE and she said, "Ranger Tam, what type of creatures do you mean?"

Ranger Tam kept walking for a bit and then he said, "Well, we'll probably see or hear a fox. And owls. And it won't be long before the bats will be darting about overhead. Majestic creatures!"

Maisie's eyes started to go all

SWIRLY

and I knew that it was because of the BATS.

So I gave Zach a nod and he took out the carton of RIBENA that we take EVERYWHERE with us in case Maisie starts to feel faint and we told her to drink it.

But then Gary Petrie said that nature was BORING and that he wanted to go back to the lodge and get in his HOT TUB. And also that he couldn't walk properly because of his SLIPPERS.

And that's when Ranger Tam stopped suddenly. So we all stopped too.

But he didn't turn round. He just stayed facing the other way for AGES.

I could feel Maisie's grip on my hand getting TIGHTER and TIGHTER.

And then VERY SLOWLY Ranger Tam started to turn round.

And then he looked at us all for a bit with a WEIRD LOOK on his face.

Then he said, "Did anyone else hear that?"

I looked at Jodi and her eyes were WIDE and I had NO IDEA what Ranger Tam was

talking about and all I could hear was the sound of my own

 HEART

beating in my chest!

Then Ranger Tam said, "I take it you all know the Legend of the Lake?"

And we all shook our heads because we **DEFINITELY** didn't.

And that's when Ranger Tam smiled and said, "Well, you'd better follow me then."

So we all followed Ranger Tam into the woods.

And everyone was SILENT and I knew
that it was because they were trying to HEAR
whatever it was Ranger Tam had heard that
obviously had something to do with the

⭐ LEGEND ⭐

OF THE

⭐ LAKE. ⭐

I listened closely but all I could hear was the
SNAPPING of branches under everyone's

feet and an OWL somewhere in the distance.

And, to be honest, I couldn't really concentrate properly because it was a LOT darker in the woods than it had been next to the lake and also because Maisie was gripping my hand so TIGHT I needed all my energy to stop myself from YELPING.

We all listened closely as Ranger Tam started talking about CRICKETS and MOTHS and MIDGES. And then he stopped and asked if anyone had any questions.

EVERYONE put up their hands but NO ONE asked about the CRICKETS or the MOTHS because everyone wanted to know about the LEGEND. And that's when Ranger Tam got a REALLY SERIOUS look on his face and said, "It's BACK."

And we all GASPED (even though we didn't know WHAT was back) because we could just TELL that it was something BAD.

Then Ranger Tam looked left. So we all looked left too. And then he looked right, so we did that too. And I had NO IDEA what we were LOOKING for but I was starting to get a bit worried that it might be a WOLF or a MASSIVE BEAR or something.

But then Ranger Tam let out a LONG SIGH and said, "I wasn't sure if your teachers were

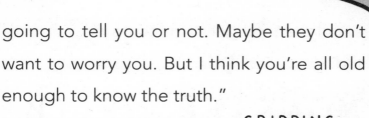

going to tell you or not. Maybe they don't want to worry you. But I think you're all old enough to know the truth."

That's when I felt someone GRIPPING my other hand and I saw that it was Jodi and also that her EYES were so WIDE they looked like they were going to POP OUT.

And then Ranger Tam took a deep breath and whispered, "It's the

MONSTER. IT'S BACK."

AND WE ALL GASPED.

And then Tam said, "Aye. You're RIGHT to gasp. And she's a big one as well! She's lived in that lake for over a hundred years!"

We all STARED at Tam as he pointed back to where the lake was and Jodi gripped my hand even TIGHTER.

And then he said, "There'd been no

sightings for a long time. To be honest with you, I thought the old girl had died. But then, just last week, I saw her with my OWN EYES."

And that's when Zach did a GULP.

And then Ranger Tam crouched down and looked us all in the eyes and said, "And, you know what, I think she's even

BIGGER

than she was before!"

And that's when we heard a SCREAM and everyone GASPED again and Maisie's hand

went LIMP in mine and she slumped to the
ground with a THUD.

And Gary Petrie started shouting, "HELP!
I'M BEING ATTACKED!"

I had

NO IDEA

what was going on and **NONE** of us could see Gary Petrie because he was too far behind us because of his **SLIPPERS**.

I looked at Jodi. And Jodi looked at me.

And I knew what she was thinking because I was thinking the **SAME THING**.

It was the

MONSTER!

"Gary, Put Some Trousers On!"

When we got out of the woods and back to the lake, no one could BELIEVE how many MIDGE BITES Gary Petrie had on his legs!

Ranger Tam said he had something back at the hotel that would help. And also that a robe and slippers had been DAFT THINGS

to wear in the woods.

But Gary wasn't listening because he was too busy COUNTING his midge bites and saying stuff like, "I'm up to TWENTY just on this leg!"

I looked at Jodi and her eyes were still WIDE and she was just sort of STARING into space and I knew that she was thinking about THE MONSTER.

I bent down to see how Maisie was coping with everything because she'd only just woken up after fainting in the woods and me and Zach had had to carry her out by an arm and leg each. But Maisie wasn't doing well at ALL. Her face had gone completely WHITE and she was mumbling, "No, no, no, no, no, no, no."

And then she sat up and said that she wanted to go back now.

So Zach said that sounded like a good idea and that we should all go back the lodge and have a cup of tea.

But Maisie shook her head and said that she didn't mean the LODGE, she meant her HOUSE, and that she didn't want to hear any more about the LAKE MONSTER.

And that's when I looked at Jodi and I could just TELL by her face that she DID want to

hear more about the LAKE MONSTER and that there was

NO WAY

she was going to let any of us go home until we found out EVERYTHING.

Zach sat down next to Maisie and held her hand and said that she shouldn't worry and that Ranger Tam might have been joking and that it had only been MIDGES that had attacked Gary Petrie's legs, not monsters.

That's when I looked at Jodi and she looked at me because we'd both seen the

EXPRESSION on Ranger Tam's face when he'd been talking about the MONSTER and we knew that there was

NO WAY

he was joking!

Then all the teachers came rushing over and Miss Jones saw Gary lying on the ground with his legs in the air counting his midge bites and she shouted, "GARY! Will you PLEASE go and put some TROUSERS on! Everyone can see RIGHT up your dressing gown!"

And that's when Gary started saying that it **WASN'T** a dressing gown, it was a **ROBE**, and also that he had **SHORTS** on underneath anyway.

Next Ranger Tam appeared with a tube of cream and told Gary to take it back to his lodge and put it on and that it would help the bites. And he also told him to put some **LOOSE TROUSERS** on so his legs didn't get too hot and make the bites more

ITCHY

Then Miss Jones came over to us because Maisie was shaking her head backwards and forwards and not moving from where we were standing.

Miss Jones looked at me before she said anything to Maisie and I knew that was because out of everyone I am probably the one who understands Maisie the MOST and can tell what she means even when she isn't using actual words to say stuff and she's only using her BODY or her EYES.

So that's when I said that Maisie had had a bit of a fright in the woods when Gary had screamed because of his legs. But I didn't say anything about the MONSTER. And when I looked at Jodi, she winked and gave me a little nod.

Suddenly Maisie GASPED and said, "Ranger Tam was RIGHT!"

But then Gary started YELLING that the cream was BURNING so Miss Jones

RUSHED over to him.

And that's when Maisie GASPED again
and I thought she was gasping about Gary's
Petrie's

BURNING LEGS

but then I noticed that she was POINTING
and STARING at something and that her
POINTING FINGER was SHAKING.

So I looked where she was pointing and
that's when I saw an old wooden sign that
said "Welcome to Lake Mentors".

And then Maisie looked at us all with

WIDE EYES and said, "The name is an ANAGRAM. Move all the letters around and it says something else."

I still couldn't see what Maisie meant because Maisie is MUCH better than me at PUZZLES and ANAGRAMS and stuff like that.

And then all of a sudden Zach gasped and said, "You're right!"

Jodi looked a bit annoyed and I knew that it was because SHE couldn't see it.

Then Zach said, "Um ... I guess Ranger Tam wasn't joking then."

And Jodi said, "Why? What? What is it?!"

And Zach gulped and said, "If you rearrange the letters in

MENTORS,

you get

MONSTER."

And I looked at Jodi and she looked at me and we both looked back at Zach because we'd just realised that the sign said, "Welcome to Lake Monster"!

BANSHEES!

Maisie looked TINY at the BIG TABLE in the hotel. And she felt so far away that I kept having to actually SHOUT so she could hear me.

None of us could BELIEVE how fancy it was inside the hotel OR how old everything

looked.

Zach said that he was pretty sure all the furniture and chairs were ANTIQUES, which meant that they were at LEAST one hundred years old, and as SOON as he said that I thought about how Ranger Tam had said the MONSTER had lived in the lake for over one hundred years.

Jodi was STARING down at the table with a really

WEIRD LOOK

on her face.

And then she looked up at me and Zach and said, "I don't know what to do."

I thought she was talking about the **MONSTER** because I felt EXACTLY THE SAME. I had

NO IDEA

what we were going to do! And I **KNEW** that there was

NO WAY

I was going to be able to SLEEP because

our cabin was RIGHT next to the lake!

But then Maisie started SMILING and she picked up one of the little forks in front of Jodi and handed it to her and Jodi smiled and said thanks.

And I saw that there were LOADS of forks and knives on the table and that I hadn't even noticed how many there were because I couldn't stop thinking about the

That's when Zach nudged me and said that he thought all the cutlery was a bit WEIRD and that the hotel was a bit CREEPY too.

Then Ranger Tam appeared and he was wearing a white apron and a CHEF'S HAT and he said, "Your first course! Enjoy!"

And then he asked us how Gary was and we pointed down the table and said that he was fine.

Then Ranger Tam said, "That one screams like a banshee! Gave me the fright of my life!"

And that's when Zach asked him what a BANSHEE was and Ranger Tam got a

SERIOUS LOOK on his face again and said, "Did your teachers not tell you about those either?"

That's when Jodi's eyes went WIDE and she said, "Tell us."

And Ranger Tam came closer and whispered, "They're wailing ghosts that live in the woods. Noisy things as well!"

And that's when the WHOLE TABLE started SHAKING and all the CUTLERY started jumping around and CLATTERING and I looked and saw that it was MAISIE causing the shaking. And I didn't BLAME

her for shaking so much because ghosts are
SCARY, especially weird, wailing ones that
live in the woods!

And even though the table was shaking, Jodi said, "Can you tell us more about the monster? We need to know."

But as soon as Ranger Tam opened his mouth, all the LIGHTS went out and

everyone SCREAMED.

When the lights came back on, Maisie was NOWHERE to be seen.

I was just about to start PANICKING when I realised what had happened and I lifted the edge of the tablecloth and saw that Maisie had fainted and slipped off her chair and landed underneath the table.

That's when Ranger Tam said, "Just a wee flicker! Happens all the time up here in the Highlands!"

But I could tell by his face that he was definitely **WORRIED** about something.

So that's when I **SIGNALLED** to Jodi and Zach to meet me under the table. And the table was **SO BIG** that the three of us were able to sit up with our legs crossed and I don't think the teachers even noticed that we were under there.

I pulled Maisie on to my lap and she kept her eyes shut but opened her hand and I

knew that meant she was waking up and that she wanted a TWIX.

So I looked at Zach but he said that he'd forgotten to bring one even though HE was supposed to be the one in charge of Maisie's FAINTING SNACKS. And then his face went a bit red and I knew he HADN'T forgotten the Twix and that he had eaten it.

But then Zach smiled and said, "Wait here."

And then he disappeared for a second and came back with a bowl of SUGAR CUBES and put one into Maisie's open hand and said, "Eat this."

And Maisie ate it in TWO SECONDS
FLAT. And then she put her hand out for
another one and Zach laughed.

That's when I said, "I've called you all here
under the dining table because we need to
have an

EMERGENCY MEETING

right away."

And Jodi nodded LOADS and she didn't
even seem ANNOYED that I had been the
one to say all the OFFICIAL STUFF about

the meeting and I knew it was because this was SERIOUS because there was a MONSTER and now there were WAILING BANSHEES too. So there wasn't any time to argue about who was in charge.

Zach said that we needed to find out MORE about the LAKE MONSTER and Jodi nodded LOADS again.

Then Zach said, "We need to find out where it LURKS so we can stay FAR away from there!"

And Maisie nodded loads too, but her eyes were still shut tight and she kept crunching on the sugar cubes.

But Jodi didn't nod this time. And I knew that it was because she didn't WANT to stay far away from it.

And that's when she said, "I think we should try to find it."

And Maisie

GASPED.

Because we could all see that Jodi had

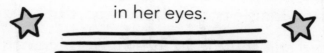

THAT LOOK

in her eyes.

The **SHINY LOOK** that she gets when she

has a

PLAN.

Noises in the Night

That night I couldn't sleep.

And it wasn't just because Maisie snores MEGA LOUD for such a small person. OR because she'd brought her giant HUMPBACK WHALE to bed with her.

It was because I could hear NOISES

outside the lodge.

Strange **SPLASHING** noises!

But I must have fallen asleep at some point because the next thing I remember was Jodi's face staring down at me from above.

I ALMOST SCREAMED

when I saw it but then Jodi put her hand over my mouth and put her finger to her lips.

That's when I woke up a bit more and calmed down and Jodi took her hand off my mouth and whispered, "Can you hear that?"

So I listened but all I could hear was Maisie snoring.

Then Jodi said, "I think there's something outside. I'm going to check."

And then she jumped off the bed and I had to literally LEAP off the bed too so I could PIN her to the ground. Because if there WAS something outside, then there was NO WAY I was letting her open the door OR go outside!

That's when I whispered, "You're not unlocking that door!"

But Jodi kept WRIGGLING and trying to get free and saying that someone needed to INVESTIGATE so I actually had to lie on TOP of her and make my body go all HEAVY like I used to do when I was little and my mum was trying to make me go somewhere I didn't want to go.

But then Jodi yelled, "OK! OK! Ouch! Get off me!"

And that woke Maisie up and she shone her torch RIGHT in our eyes and said, "What's going on? What are you both DOING down there?!"

But before I could explain, Jodi said, "SHHHHHHH! There it is again. Listen!"

And that's when I realised that Jodi hadn't

meant the SPLASHING sound that I'd heard before I fell asleep.

Because this wasn't a splashing sound at ALL.

It was WORSE.

And that's when Maisie said, "Is …is …is that WAILING?!"

And we nodded because there was no point trying to hide it because it obviously WAS wailing.

And that's when Maisie's eyes went WIDE and she whispered,

"BANSHEE!"

By the time we got to the boys' lodge, Maisie was shaking SO MUCH that I had to check she wasn't FREEZING TO DEATH and that she was just shaking with FEAR.

That's when Jodi turned to us and said, "The wailing is definitely coming from here."

And she was right. The wailing was much LOUDER now and I could hardly BREATHE because I couldn't believe there was a

BANSHEE.

That's when Jodi said, "I think it might be inside. I'm going in."

But then Maisie's eyes went WIDE and she pointed to something and started WHIMPERING.

And that's when I looked and saw MIST coming from behind the boys' lodge and I actually GULPED because I have a

WILD IMAGINATION

and I was imagining a weird MISTY GHOST THING making all the noise!

That's when Jodi took a DEEP BREATH and started TALKING TO HERSELF, saying things like "Stay CALM" and "This is what you've been TRAINING FOR" because Jodi wants to be an actual GHOST HUNTER when she's older and she watches all the EXTREME HAUNTING programmes on TV with her mum and she doesn't even get SCARED.

So that's when I said, "What are we going to do if we see it?!"

Jodi said, "I'm going to take a VIDEO of it on Maisie's phone to prove that ghosts EXIST. And then I'll probably call the police and the government."

And I nodded because I didn't really know what else to do because things were getting a bit

OUT OF CONTROL

with the LAKE MONSTER and the scary BANSHEE GHOST!

But then the wailing got LOUDER and there was LOADS of mist and Jodi hissed

"NOW!" and then she RAN behind the lodge towards the

BANSHEE.

Me and Maisie just stood still because my feet wouldn't work and also because Maisie was lying in the grass because she'd fainted.

But then I heard JODI scream and I realised that I was going to have to leave Maisie and save Jodi from the BANSHEE.

I RACED around the corner and that's when I found Jodi standing with her hand over her mouth and she had her EYES CLOSED.

So I looked through the mist and that's when I saw something. But it wasn't a BANSHEE. It was GARY PETRIE. And he was sitting in his HOT TUB. And it didn't look like he had any CLOTHES on!

And then he started WAILING.

That's when Gary said that his bites had been so SORE and ITCHY that he'd got out of bed to see if the hot tub would help but it hadn't and that it had made them MUCH WORSE.

And that's when Gary said, "Pass me my robe."

And Jodi kept her eyes shut tight and said,

"NO WAY!"

Then Gary said, "I'm not naked! I've got my shorts on!"

But Jodi still wouldn't open her eyes just in case.

So I found Gary's robe and I picked it up

and threw it at him.

But there was a splash and Gary said,
"Awww, Izzy! You've SOAKED IT!"

So that's when I told Gary to

HURRY UP

because I had to get back to Maisie because
she'd fainted on the grass and was just
LYING there on the grass without us. And
that's when Gary LEAPED out of the hot tub
and ran past us in the soaking-wet robe and
I knew that he was going to check if Maisie
was OK.

But then he yelled, "Where is she? I can't see her."

And that's when I got a horrible feeling in my stomach (which always happens just before I start to panic). So I took a deep breath and looked round the corner at the spot where I'd left Maisie.

But she was

GONE.

MAISIE'S MISSING!

Me, Jodi and Gary ran around the boys' lodge in a big circle but we couldn't see Maisie.

Then Gary said, "Maybe she woke up and went inside. I'm going to check."

And that's when Jodi **GRABBED** my arm

and declared a **SUPER-FAST**

EMERGENCY MEETING.

And I nodded **LOADS** because I knew it had to be fast because we needed to find Maisie

ASAP,

and also because Gary wasn't allowed to be part of it because only me and Jodi and Maisie and Zach are allowed to be part of

79

our meetings and INVESTIGATIONS.

That's when Jodi said that she thought Maisie's disappearance might have something to do with the MONSTER and that we needed to go and find Ranger Tam NOW. She said that we couldn't save Maisie unless we knew more about it.

Just then Gary BURST out of the boys' lodge and said she wasn't inside. "We need to do a MANHUNT and we need to do it NOW. I've woken up Zach to help. Let's go!"

And that's when Jodi got REALLY annoyed and she said, "Hey! YOU don't decide how WE find Maisie. WE do. She's

OUR friend and this is OUR investigation."

And that's when Gary's eyebrows went REALLY HIGH and he said, "What investigation?"

And Jodi got a look on her face and it was because she knew that she'd said

TOO MUCH.

That's when Gary pulled the tie on his robe really tight and then he put his hands on his hips like JODI does and said, "Well. Maisie is MY friend, too. Maybe even my girlfriend! So I'm part of this now. Like it or not."

And I thought Jodi was going to

SCREAM WITH ANGER

like the time when she had clearly **WON** the egg-and-spoon race at school sports' day but the judge hadn't been paying attention and gave the medal to someone **ELSE**.

But Jodi **DIDN'T** scream. She just said, "Fine. You and Zach keep looking for Maisie. Me and Izzy need to go and do something

URGENTLY."

And then before I could say anything, Jodi
grabbed my hand and we were running
away from the lake and the lodges and up
towards the hotel.

When we got to the big hotel doors, I thought they would be locked. But they weren't.

So we went inside and that's when we saw most of the lights were still on in the hall and up the staircase.

I looked at the big clock at the bottom of the stairs and I said, "It's almost midnight. Ranger Tam will have gone home."

But Jodi shook her head and said that she'd heard Ranger Tam tell the teachers that he was available "24/7" if they needed any help and just to come to the reception and he'd be there.

So that's when I said, "Well, he's not here

tonight."

But then Jodi said, "Look!"

And she pointed and I saw that there was a fancy gold bell on the reception desk.

So I reached out my hand and gave it a

DING

and waited. But no one came.

So Jodi reached out and gave it TWO dings. But that didn't work either.

But then I heard something so I walked over towards the staircase and I saw a door that was slightly open and I heard a voice from inside say, "I'm a bit worried about the boat tour tonight."

So I waved Jodi over.

Then we heard Ranger Tam say, "Don't worry. I won't get as close as I did last time."

And the other voice said, "You'd better not! You almost touched the tail!"

I looked at Jodi and she looked at me because we both KNEW that they were talking about the MONSTER'S TAIL.

And then all of a sudden the door opened

properly and we saw Ranger Tam and the woman who ran the hotel standing there.

That's when Ranger Tam said, "And just what are you two doing here at this hour?"

And as soon as he said that, the woman looked at her watch and hurried off without saying anything.

So that's when Jodi said, "We came to find you. We need to know

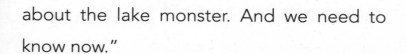

about the lake monster. And we need to know now."

That's when Ranger Tam laughed and then he said, "Well, you're out of luck, lass. I'm afraid you've caught me at a bad time. I'm just about to take the boat out."

And Jodi said, "We just need half an hour. Forty-five minutes max."

Then Ranger Tam laughed again and said, "We don't call it the Midnight Tour for nothing! It starts at midnight and I'm the captain! So unless you want to come with me—"

And before Ranger Tam could even finish his sentence, Jodi said, "YES. We'll come."

And I GASPED because there was

NO WAY I was going out in a BOAT at MIDNIGHT on to a

CREEPY LAKE

that had a MONSTER with a TAIL in it!

But then Ranger Tam laughed again and said, "Hmm. Something tells me your teachers wouldn't be too happy if I took you out on the boat at this hour! Let's go. I'll walk you back down to the lodges. We can talk on the way."

So we followed Ranger Tam out of the hotel and down towards the lodges and as soon as we started walking Jodi asked him about the BOAT and why he was taking it out at MIDNIGHT and I knew that she was asking because of what we had overheard about the TAIL.

And that's when Ranger Tam explained more about the

MIDNIGHT TOUR

of the lake he did for the guests. "There's been a LOT of recent sightings of the monster in the lake at night," he said. "People have been coming from far and wide to stay here in the hope that they'll catch a glimpse of the big lass! Everyone wants to be the first one to get a decent photo of our monster and get themselves in the newspaper. Or maybe even on TV!"

So that's when I said, "How do you know the monster is a girl?"

And Ranger Tam looked a bit surprised and he said, "Well. Um … I suppose I don't!"

That's when Jodi asked what ELSE he could tell us about the monster. Like what it LOOKED LIKE. And I noticed that she'd started walking REALLY SLOWLY and I knew that it was because she wanted us to

get as much INFORMATION as possible before we got to the lodges.

And that's when Ranger Tam said, "Well, she's a scary-looking one, I'll tell you that!"

And then he laughed for ages even though it wasn't funny at ALL.

Then he said, "It's her long tail that's been spotted the most. I've seen it myself. Long, green and SLIMY! Gives me the shivers just THINKING about it."

And he chuckled to himself again.

I had no idea why he kept laughing because

a **GIANT** MONSTER

living in the lake with a **LONG SLIMY TAIL**
definitely wasn't funny. But then I realised
that he was probably just a nervous laugher
like my mum.

So anyway, then Jodi asked about the
HEAD, but Ranger Tam said that sightings
of the monster's head were **VERY RARE**
but that he had a **FEELING** there might be

one soon.

Jodi asked him why he thought that and Ranger Tam said, "Because she's been getting CLOSER."

That's when I remembered what the hotel lady had said so I said, "You almost touched the tail with your boat."

And Ranger Tam looked a bit surprised so I had to explain that we'd overheard him talking.

And then Ranger Tam got a bit of a

WEIRD LOOK

on his face and he stopped walking and said, "Oh? And what else did you hear, lass?"

But I said that we hadn't heard anything else and then Jodi asked about the sightings again and what people had told him.

Ranger Tam smiled and started walking again and said, "We've heard

LOTS

of things recently. There's been over twenty sightings in the past two weeks alone! Some guests have even spotted the monster having a midnight swim right outside their

lodge windows. Can you believe it?"

And that's when I heard myself GULP because I knew that he probably meant OUR window!

That's when Jodi said, "What does the monster look like? What do people say who've seen it?"

Ranger Tam stopped again and said, "Look, lass. Are you sure you want to know all this? I mean, it's pretty frightening stuff!"

Jodi nodded. And then Ranger Tam looked at me and I nodded too, even though I wasn't really sure if I **DID** want to hear but I knew Jodi would be annoyed at me if I didn't nod.

Then Ranger Tam said, "Well, most people who have seen the monster say it's got a massive long green tail. Some even say it looks a bit like a dinosaur. But there's one thing they **ALL** say –

  THAT IT'S TERRIFYING!"

And then Tam lowered his voice and looked at us with a

 SERIOUS FACE

and said, "I don't know if I should tell you this or not, but there's actually been a couple of LAND SIGHTINGS. Couldn't believe it when I heard. Never heard of it on land before in all my days. Everyone's always thought the monster could only survive in water."

And that's when Jodi's eyes went WIDE and she looked at me and I looked at her because we were both worried that the monster had come on to land and taken MAISIE.

We asked why he thought it would come ashore now.

And that's when Ranger Tam's eyes went

WIDE this time and he said, "Well, if you want my opinion, there's only one explanation." And his eyes went even **WIDER** and he said, "I think she's

HUNGRY!"

When we got back to the lake, I could hardly **BREATHE** because we'd run so fast.

As soon as Ranger Tam had said about the monster being **HUNGRY**, I'd grabbed Jodi's hand and we'd **RUN** all the way back.

I could feel my heart POUNDING in my ears and it wasn't just because of the RUNNING, it was because I was TERRIFIED that the LAKE MONSTER had EATEN MAISIE.

I was just about to say that we needed to wake Miss Jones and tell her that Maisie might have been EATEN when Jodi said, "LOOK!"

And I looked and saw WEIRD MARKS in the mud at our feet. Jodi took

her **TORCH** out of her pocket and shone it on the ground, and I **GASPED** because the weird marks went all the way from where we were standing and into the lake.

That's when Jodi said, "They're tracks. And whatever made them is

BIG."

And then Jodi looked up at me and her eyes were **HUGE** and she said, "I think they might be **TAIL TRACKS.**"

And that's when we both heard a SPLASH a few metres away and I gasped and grabbed Jodi's arm and made her drop the torch. Jodi quickly picked it up and pointed it at the water but there was nothing there except a few ripples.

That's when Jodi whispered, "That was it! It's in there!"

And I nodded. And I kept nodding for ages because I sort of couldn't STOP because I was

FREAKING OUT

because the monster had obviously just been RIGHT outside our cabin!

Jodi turned to me and said, "We must have missed it by SECONDS!"

And that's when we heard a voice say, "Missed what?"

And we spun round and saw MAISIE!

I grabbed Maisie and hugged her for AGES.

And then Zach said that he and Gary Petrie had found her in our lodge.

And then Zach looked at Jodi and said, "Didn't you check there?"

But Jodi didn't say anything because we

HADN'T checked there and I knew that Jodi felt a bit silly because I did too.

That's when Maisie said that she'd woken up and, when she couldn't see us, she'd run back to our lodge and locked the door and used the phone in the lodge to call Zach on his mobile. I was

to see Maisie that I kept hugging and hugging her and she kept giggling and saying, "Not so tight!"

Then Gary Petrie said that he was going

back to bed before Mr Beattie woke up and found out that they'd left the lodge because he didn't want to get into trouble and not be allowed to do the

RAFT BUILDING

in the morning.

And Zach said that he was going too but Jodi said, "Hold on a second, Zach. We need to have meeting. A pretty serious one."

And that's when Maisie squeezed me back and she squeezed so hard I actually SCREAMED a bit and that made HER scream and suddenly the lights in all the lodges went on and Gary Petrie hissed, "Run back to your lodge.

GO!."

So we all ran.

On Camera

REALLY EARLY the next morning there was a knock at our cabin door.

I sat up RIGHT AWAY and that's when I saw that Jodi and Maisie were still fast asleep and that Jodi had her mouth WIDE open and that she was DROOLING.

So I looked at the clock and it said 5.55am so I lay back down because I thought I must have DREAMED the knock because it didn't make any sense that someone would be knocking at the lodge door at that time.

But then there was a knock at the WINDOW next to our bed and a voice said, "It's me. Let me in!"

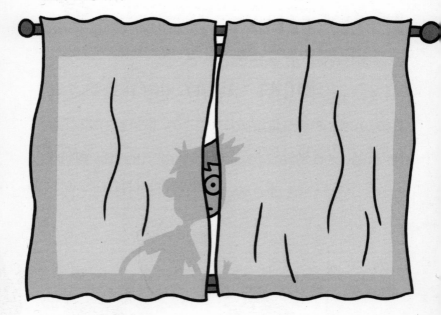

And I jumped up and opened the bedroom curtains a bit and saw that it was Zach.

So I got up and unlocked the door and let him in and explained that Jodi and Maisie were still sleeping because of the

 LATE NIGHT.

That's when Zach said, "I can't sleep. I need to know what's going on. You found out more, didn't you? About the lake monster? That's why Jodi wanted to have a meeting late last night, isn't it?"

I was just about to say yes when a voice behind me said, "Please tell me it's good news!"

And I turned and saw Maisie in her pyjamas and she was squeezing her HUMPBACK WHALE so much it looked like his EYE was going to POP OUT.

So I said that it was time to wake up Jodi so we could have an

OFFICIAL MEETING.

And I said it because I knew we couldn't

have a meeting that was THIS serious without all FOUR of us being there and also because I didn't want to be the one to tell Maisie that the lake monster had been sighted ON LAND, looking for FOOD, and that it had been RIGHT outside our cabin last night!

So I went and got Jodi and told her that we were waiting for her to do the meeting and she

LEAPED

out of bed and ran into the living room.

And Zach actually GASPED when he saw her because her hair was ALL OVER THE PLACE and she was still wearing her giant BEDTIME BRACES.

Then Jodi said, "We found out more about the monster last night."

And that's when I looked at Zach and nodded and he nodded back and moved a bit closer to Maisie and held his arms out a bit in case she fainted.

And that's when I explained about Ranger Tam and the Midnight Tour and all the SIGHTINGS there had been in the past couple of weeks. And how Ranger Tam had almost touched the monster's tail with his boat!

And then I looked at Jodi because I didn't want to be the one to say the next bit in case it made Maisie scream and also because I was starting to feel a bit DIZZY myself because I couldn't believe we were having a conversation about an

ACTUAL MONSTER.

Jodi took a deep breath and said, "The lake monster doesn't stay in the lake. It can come on land too."

Zach looked at Jodi and then at me and then back at Jodi and then he said, "Does it have legs? Does it slide like a crocodile?"

I looked at Maisie because I thought she

was going to start

FREAKING OUT

but she was just sitting there with her mouth wide open, staring at Zach. And I knew that it was because she was in SHOCK.

We explained that no one had known it could come on land and that it was a new thing.

And then Zach said, "Why is it coming on land all of a sudden then? Is there something wrong with the water?"

And Jodi looked at me and I looked at

Jodi and then we both looked back at Zach.

Jodi said, "Ranger Tam said he thinks it's because the monster is HUNGRY. He thinks it's coming on land to look for food."

And Zach's eyes went WIDE.

And that's when Maisie jumped up and screamed,

"I WANT TO GO HOME RIGHT NOW!!!"

Once we eventually got Maisie to stop SHAKING, Jodi said that we all needed to be CALM and that this was a

ONCE IN A LIFETIME

opportunity and that we were LUCKY.

And that's when Zach's voice went all high and he said, "LUCKY?!"

Jodi NODDED. And she even SMILED a bit too!

And that's when she said that she had an EXCITING PROPOSAL for us. And she was smiling SO MUCH that it was really starting to

FREAK ME OUT.

That's when I started to worry that she was maybe still ASLEEP and that she was doing some sort of weird

SLEEPWALKING thing.

Or that maybe she was so tired that she was DELIRIOUS, which is when you go a bit WEIRD and HYPER and start to SEE

THINGS that aren't there because you're not well and you've got a **TEMPERATURE**.

So I put my hand on Jodi's head but it didn't feel hot or sweaty. But I made her sit down anyway and drink a glass of water.

When she was finished, she seemed a little bit calmer so I asked her what she meant about the

AMAZING OPPORTUNITY

and the **EXCITING PROPOSAL**. And that's when she started smiling again but it wasn't as creepy this time.

And then she said, "I want us to be the FIRST PEOPLE EVER to prove that there's a MONSTER in the lake!"

And she made her EYES go really WIDE.

Then she said, "We'd be FAMOUS."

And that's when Zach started smiling a bit, too. And I knew that it was because becoming FAMOUS is something he really wants to do. And I know that for a FACT because I saw it on his BUCKET LIST when we had a supply teacher once and she made

us write one ALL DAY and we didn't do any maths OR literacy and by the end of the day everyone's BUCKET LISTS were HUGE.

So anyway, Jodi said that because we were staying in the lodge RIGHT next to the lake that we had more chance than ANYONE of spotting the LAKE MONSTER and taking a CLEAR PHOTOGRAPH of it. And we might even be able to take a VIDEO of it on Zach's phone.

And that's when Zach said, "I accept your proposal. Let's catch the monster on CAMERA!"

And Jodi smiled LOADS.

And then she looked at me but I said that I wasn't sure because it sounded

DANGEROUS.

But then Jodi said that we were already at the centre of the

DANGER ZONE

and also that if we were the first ones EVER to prove that the lake monster legend was TRUE, then we'd probably get a million pounds or a book deal or a trip to Disneyland or something from the Queen.

So I took a deep breath and said, "OK. I'm in."

And Jodi grabbed me and gave me a hug and she hardly EVER does that so I knew she was really happy.

And then we all looked at Maisie.

But Maisie was face down on the rug.

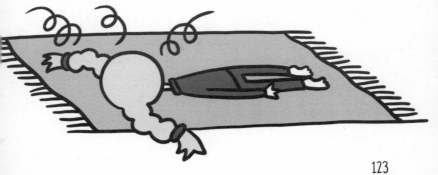

Raft
Building

It was CHAOS when we got to the raft-building station.

Ranger Tam wasn't there yet and Miss Jones and Mr Beattie were trying to find RAFT-BUILDING INSTRUCTIONS on their phones and EVERYONE was pushing these barrels around and trying to knock each other over with them.

Jodi was getting  **MEGA** STRESSED because she said she wanted to be the first one on the water in case the **MONSTER** was around so we could take a photograph but she couldn't figure out how to get the barrels to stay together.

That's when Gary Petrie appeared and asked if we'd like some help but Jodi said no because Jodi doesn't like help and she's not

very good at working with others when we do TEAM ACTIVITIES because she always wants to do everything herself because she thinks she can do it better.

And that's when Gary did a bit of a weird

HEAD-TILT THING

and said, "You suuuuure?"

And then he kept doing the weird head-tilt thing and I thought that maybe he had a BLOCKED EAR from being in his hot tub or something.

But then he cleared his throat and said,

"**AHEM**. I'm just saying. It's fine if you don't want my help but you **MIGHT** want to take a look over **THERE**."

And then we realised that Gary was tilting his head because he wanted us to see something, so we all looked and that's when we saw that he'd actually **FINISHED** building his raft.

Jodi took one look at it and said, "Good luck. That'll sink in under FIVE SECONDS."

And that's when Gary Petrie GASPED and said that it WOULD NOT and that he had used even MORE barrels than he was meant to.

And Jodi rolled her eyes and said, "Exactly!"

And that's when Gary Petrie

CHALLENGED

us to a RAFT-OFF, and I was just about to say NO because we had a MONSTER to think about when Jodi yelled, "FINE. Let's DO THIS."

I looked at Zach and he was shaking his head because we both KNEW that Jodi was about to get

OUT OF CONTROL.

We watched as Jodi started running around, pulling at ropes and telling us what to do and then telling us to do it FASTER and BETTER and that there was NO WAY Gary Petrie was going to build a better raft than US.

So that's when I pointed out that we should be focusing on **OTHER THINGS** and then I gave Jodi a **LOOK**.

And that's when Ranger Tam appeared and he said, "What do you call this?! Right. Let's get these rafts fixed and get you lot on that lake!"

And then he clapped his hands so loudly that Maisie **YELPED**.

Jodi almost **LEAPED** on Ranger Tam, saying she needed to ask him

SEVERAL QUESTIONS ASAP.

He laughed out loud and that made Maisie yelp AGAIN. And then he said, "More questions?! Well, I need to get these rafts sorted first and then I'll see if I can help you, lass, OK?"

But I could tell by the look on Jodi's face that she was definitely NOT OK with it. And so could Ranger Tam.

So that's when he said, "Right, well. Looks like you lot have finished your raft so why don't you come with me to help the others? You can ask me your questions while we work."

And then Ranger Tam pointed at Maisie

and said, "What's the wee lass doing?"

And we saw that Maisie was standing on a box looking through Jodi's BINOCULARS.

So that's when Zach said, "She's looking out for the monster."

And Ranger Tam nodded and said, "Good lass. Keep watch! Let us know if you see anything!"

So me, Jodi and Zach followed Ranger Tam over to the TEACHERS' RAFT because that one was the WORST and Mr Beattie looked a bit like he was going to cry and Miss Jones had given up and was just lying down on the ground taking big gulps from her water bottle.

So we helped Ranger Tam fix the teachers' raft and Zach asked him if the monster had LEGS or if it SLID AROUND on the ground. And Ranger Tam said that he was sure the monster could WALK ON TWO LEGS because he'd spotted GIANT FOOTPRINTS next to the lake.

And then he pointed just a few metres from where we were standing and said, "Right there. I spotted them this morning actually, when I was setting up the raft building. Great big feet, it's got."

I **GASPED** and Zach's mouth fell **WIDE OPEN** because Ranger Tam was pointing to a spot **RIGHT** outside our lodge!

Then Jodi asked if there had been any **SIGHTINGS** of the **MONSTER** on the **MIDNIGHT TOUR** the night before. And I knew that she wanted to know because she wanted **US** to be the first ones to get **PHOTOGRAPHIC EVIDENCE**.

And Tam shook his head and said, "No sightings last night, no. Not sure where she

got to! I had a lot of disappointed folk on board. But I'll take them out again tonight. I've got a funny feeling we might get a good view of her later."

Then he grabbed loads of LIFE JACKETS for us and made us all sit quietly for AGES while he explained the LAKE SAFETY RULES. And that's when I realised what we were ACTUALLY DOING. We were ACTUALLY going to float on a RAFT on a LAKE that had a one-hundred-year-old giant MONSTER living in it!

And I knew that I had to sit down. But before I could actually sit down I was LYING

down and everyone was standing around
me.

I had

what was going on and that's when Jodi said,
"Are you OK? You fainted!"

And then Maisie handed me a carton of Ribena and I didn't really want it but I took it anyway because I think I was in

SHOCK

because I have only fainted three times in my life including then.

That's when Miss Jones said I should go back to the lodge but I said that I was fine and that the juice was helping because it was.

Miss Jones made me sit down at the side and Maisie sat with me and we watched while everyone else got ready to go out on the rafts. And Maisie held my hand and she kept patting it like I do to hers when she faints.

Then when everyone was ready to go out on the lake, Jodi and Zach came over to us and Jodi gave me another hug!

And then she said, "If anything happens to us, you can have my survival outfit. You might need it."

And then she took a deep breath and walked towards the lake.

"IT'S A TAIL!"

As **SOON** as Jodi and Zach started to climb on to the raft, Maisie said, "I'm going, too. Will you be **OK** without me, Izzy?"

I was **SHOCKED** because I thought Maisie would be **TERRIFIED** to go out on the lake because of the **MONSTER**. But she said,

139

"Two isn't enough if something goes wrong. They might need me."

And that's when I realised that if MAISIE could be brave even when we had a LAKE MONSTER to deal with, then I could be, too.

So that's when I said that I was coming as well and Maisie smiled and we ran towards the lake and yelled, "Wait for us!"

Ranger Tam put our life jackets on and double-checked that we'd remembered ALL the rules and then he made us answer QUESTIONS about the rules and when we got them all right he said, "OK. Let's get you

on the raft."

As soon as we got on the raft, Jodi looked across at Gary and yelled,

"GO!"

And that's when I realised that Jodi wanted us to RACE Gary.

So we all started using our paddles but we must have been doing it wrong because we kept going in CIRCLES rather than forward.

That's when Gary Petrie's raft pushed RIGHT past ours and he SPLASHED us with his paddle ON PURPOSE and yelled,

"SEE YOU LATER, AMIGOS!" And then he started laughing REALLY LOUD and all FAKE.

That's when Zach said that we all needed to stop paddling, so we did.

And then he said, "On the count of three, we're all going to start again at the same time and do it like THIS, OK?"

And then Zach did a demonstration and that's when I realised that it was MY fault that we had been going round in circles because I'd been paddling BACKWARDS by mistake and Maisie had been copying me.

So as soon as Zach counted to three we all started paddling again the RIGHT WAY and the raft started to move forward and Jodi yelled, "THAT'S IT! KEEP IT UP

IN THE BACK!"

I looked at Maisie because WE were the back and Maisie's little arms were going so fast I wasn't sure how long she was going to be able to keep paddling!

Then I looked up and saw that Gary's raft was WAY ahead of us and so were all the other rafts.

But then all of a sudden Zach STOPPED paddling.

And Jodi said, "ZACH!"

But Zach didn't answer.

And we all watched the paddle slip RIGHT out of his hand and into the lake!

And that's when I shouted, "Zach! Grab it!"

But Zach DIDN'T grab it.

He didn't even MOVE.

He just said, "What's THAT?!"

And I leaned over and looked where he was looking and that's when I GASPED because there was a long, thick GREEN THING with SPIKY BITS on it floating right beside us!

Zach yelled, "It's a tail, isn't it?! IT'S A TAIL!"

Then he started

SQUEALING

and I didn't blame him because it WAS a tail and it obviously belonged to the MONSTER.

And then Jodi started yelling, "WHERE'S THE REST OF IT?"

But I could only see the tail and I knew that that could only mean ONE THING.

I looked at Maisie and her eyes were

WIDE WITH FEAR.

And that's when I said, "Maisie, listen to me VERY CAREFULLY. Whatever you do, DON'T FAINT!"

And Maisie nodded loads and started doing her MEDITATION BREATHING EXERCISES.

Because I knew that there was only ONE place the monster could be.

It was underneath our RAFT.

Hot
Tub
Pizza

We all sat frozen in our seats, waiting for Ranger Tam to come over. Jodi had managed to get his attention by waving an **EMERGENCY FLAG** in the air that she'd taken from her **SURVIVAL SUIT**.

As **SOON** as Ranger Tam paddled over

and saw what WE were looking at, his face went

WHITE WITH FEAR.

And that's when Zach started

FREAKING OUT!

Before we could do anything, he fell off the raft and into the lake!

Zach was splashing EVERYWHERE and

that's when Jodi looked at us and said,

"HOLD ON TO MY LEGS. NOW!"

And even though it was CHAOS, I grabbed Jodi's legs and so did Maisie and we held on TIGHT while Jodi leaned over the raft.

And then she yelled,

"ZACH! GRAB THE OAR. I'LL PULL YOU IN."

But Zach wasn't listening because he was
PANICKING.

And then he started screaming,

 "THERE'S SOMETHING

UNDER MY FEET!

I'M STANDING ON

SOMETHING!"

And I looked around as much as I could while I held on to Jodi's leg but I couldn't see the tail ANYWHERE.

I looked at Maisie and she looked at me and I could see

in her face and I knew that there was probably

on MY face too because we both knew that we'd just seen the MONSTER'S TAIL and that Zach was probably STANDING on it RIGHT NOW.

But then Ranger Tam shouted, "Zach! Listen to me. That's the BOTTOM OF THE LAKE you can feel. Stand up. "

And Zach stopped splashing and stood up and that's when we saw that the water was only up to his WAIST.

Zach looked a bit SURPRISED and then he said, "Oh, yeah."

And then Jodi helped him climb back on to the raft. And when he sat down, we all saw that he didn't look like he'd looked before he went into the water and we kept telling him how weird his FACE and EYES looked and asking him if was OK.

And that's when Maisie said, "It's because he saw the monster.

It's  CHANGED him."

And Zach nodded a bit and said that he was in shock, but we already knew that because it was obvious.

So that's when Ranger Tam started acting a bit PANICKED and said it was time to get back to shore. And then he told all the other rafts to turn back.

That's when Gary Petrie said that it was RUBBISH because we'd only just got on the rafts and that Zach was FINE and the water wasn't even that COLD.

Then Gary put his arm in the water to show everyone that it wasn't cold and that's when Maisie shouted,

"NO! DON'T!"

And Gary gasped and pulled his hand out of the lake RIGHT AWAY.

And I looked at Jodi and Jodi looked at me because it hadn't just been MAISIE that had shouted "NO! DON'T!"

Ranger Tam had shouted it too!

And Ranger Tam looked

TERRIFIED.

The Shed Monster

As soon as we got back to the lodge Jodi called an

EMERGENCY MEETING.

Zach had changed into some clothes that weren't wet but he was still shivering and that's when Jodi said that we needed a **TINFOIL BLANKET** to wrap round him to get him warm **ASAP**. But we didn't have any tinfoil in the lodge so Maisie just wrapped loads of normal blankets round him and that helped.

I was watching Ranger Tam from the Big Window because even though he'd sent us all back to the lodges, he was still on a raft out on the lake, peering into the water. And I knew that he was looking for the MONSTER.

That's when Jodi said, "The secret meeting has officially begun." And she took a deep breath and said, "I think we can all agree this is probably the most SERIOUS problem we've ever had to deal with."

And we all nodded.

Then Jodi said, "Zach was almost eaten by a lake monster today."

And me and Maisie both GASPED because even though that was definitely TRUE, we hadn't been expecting Jodi to

say it (especially right in front of ZACH who was clearly still in SHOCK)!

I looked at Zach to see if he was OK and that's when I saw that his head was sort of slumped to the side and that he was leaning against Maisie and also that he had fainted.

Then all of a sudden there was a loud knock at the door and Maisie squealed.

Jodi looked at me but I just shrugged because I didn't know who it was.

And then Maisie squeaked a bit and we looked and saw that Zach was actually LYING on top of her now so that she was squashed against the side of the couch.

So we pulled Zach off and that's when he woke up and started SHAKING again and saying, "What's happening?! What's happening?!"

And that's when we heard Gary Petrie yell, "It's me! GP!"

And Jodi rolled her eyes and said, "GO AWAY, GARY! WE'RE BUSY!"

But then Gary KNOCKED AGAIN and yelled, "I've got lunch for us all at my lodge to say sorry for moaning about Zach falling in the water. Is he OK?"

That's when my stomach started RUMBLING and I realised that none of

us had even eaten breakfast because of everything that was going on.

And then Maisie said, "I'm hungry."

And I could tell that Jodi wanted to keep doing the secret meeting but then HER stomach rumbled TOO. And she yelled, "Do you have any foil at your lodge?"

And Gary laughed and said, "It's GP's lodge! We have

EVERYTHING."

I couldn't BELIEVE how big it was inside the boys' lodge. They had a MASSIVE kitchen and it was so big that the POOL TABLE was in it.

That's when Gary said, "Zach, you can take a dip in my hot tub if you want to warm up?"

And Zach nodded that he did want that. And Maisie said that Zach still looked a bit pale and that maybe she should get changed into her COSTUME and get in too in case he fainted again.

That's when Gary said that we could ALL get in the hot tub if we wanted and that he'd get Jonathan to serve us lunch there.

And that's when I looked at Jodi and back at Gary because I had

who Jonathan was because there wasn't anyone in our class called Jonathan and I didn't understand why someone called Jonathan would be serving us anything.

Then all of a sudden a door opened in the kitchen and a man wearing a CHEF'S OUTFIT came out and put loads of plates down on the kitchen table and said, "Mr Petrie, your pizza is still cooking. I'll bring it out shortly."

And Gary nodded and said, "Thank you, Jonathan."

I looked at Jodi and she had her mouth **WIDE OPEN**.

We all **STARED** as Jonathan disappeared back into the kitchen and Gary took off the **SILVER DOME** covering one of the big plates and that's when we saw that Jonathan had made

EVERY TYPE OF SANDWICH

that you can probably get!

Then Gary explained that the lakeside lodges came with PRIVATE CHEFS and that he'd read about it in the WELCOME PACK and that Jonathan had been making him LOADS of food and that he'd even made him a

CHEESEBURGER AT MIDNIGHT!

That's when I got really annoyed with myself for not reading the WELCOME PACK and I was starting to wonder if there was maybe a

HOT TUB at our lodge somewhere too!

Then Gary said, "I wasn't sure what everyone would like, and I know Jodi's a bit weird with a lot of food, so—"

And that's when Jodi interrupted Gary and said, "I am not WEIRD with food, GARY. I'm a VEGETARIAN. I've told you THAT about a million times!"

But Gary wasn't really listening because he was too busy pointing at all the sandwiches and saying, "Chicken and bacon, mozzarella and tomato, three cheeses, and Coronation chicken – without raisins, obviously!"

And I couldn't BELIEVE how FANCY

everything was because I have never SEEN sandwiches piled up in such a fancy way on a big silver tray before and it looked AMAZING!

And then Gary said, "Please note all the crusts have been removed at my request. ENJOY!"

I didn't understand why Gary was talking so WEIRD all of a sudden but I didn't really care because I was STARVING and the sandwiches looked DELICIOUS.

So we all started eating them

and Jodi said it was actually the MOST sandwiches she'd eaten in ages and that there were LOADS of vegetarian ones!

Then Gary looked at me and WINKED and I knew that it was because he HAD remembered about Jodi being a vegetarian and that he'd probably ordered loads of sandwiches especially for Jodi and that he'd just been winding her up because he likes to do that.

But then I noticed that Zach wasn't really eating and that he'd only had a tiny bite of one ham sandwich and then put it back down.

So I asked him if he was feeling OK and he said that he wasn't sure and that it was hard having a

NEAR-DEATH
EXPERIENCE

and then eating a sandwich.

And Maisie nodded LOADS and said that that's how she felt ALL THE TIME especially when really scary stuff happened like the time she saw a GIANT SEAGULL.

And that's when Gary looked at us and

said, "Am I missing something?"

And Maisie looked at Jodi and did WIDE EYES but Jodi just shook her head and reached for another sandwich. But then Maisie PULLED the sandwiches away so Jodi couldn't reach them. And then did even WIDER EYES at Jodi.

And I knew that Maisie wanted Jodi to let Gary IN on our

INVESTIGATION.

We've done that before if we've needed his help, like the time with the PHANTOM

LOLLIPOP MAN (but Jodi wasn't very happy about it).

Jodi says we need to keep a TIGHT CIRCLE when things like YETIS and DEMON DINNER LADIES and VAMPIRE RATS attack our school so that we have the best chance of

SURVIVAL.

But then Gary got up and said, "Why don't we all discuss this further in the hot tub? Jonathan can bring us some lemonade."

And that's when Jodi tapped her fingers

on the table for a bit.

And then she said, "Well. That might be OK, I suppose. And did Jonathan say something about a pizza?"

Zach said he felt MUCH better once we were eating pizza in the hot tub. And that it was

probably the most RELAXED he had felt in AGES.

Gary said he was probably going to get a hot tub in his garden when he got home so that he could relax after being at school all day.

But the person who was enjoying the hot tub most was DEFINITELY Jodi.

And she kept GIGGLING when Gary turned up the BUBBLES and Jodi NEVER giggles!

That's when Maisie said that she really liked Jonathan and that he was very helpful and nice. And Gary said that he WAS and that he was going to miss him when we went home and that he was going to see if he could get his mum to put a chocolate on his pillow before bed like Jonathan did.

And Maisie GASPED and I KNEW that she was going to ask her mum about the

CHOCOLATE-
PILLOW THING

as SOON as she got home too.

Then Jonathan appeared again with a tray

of drinks and they looked AMAZING and they had bits of PINEAPPLE on the side and CHERRIES and EVERYTHING!

Gary took a sip of one and said, "Delicious mocktail! Bravo, Jonathan!"

And Jonathan laughed and went back into the lodge.

I didn't really know what a MOCKTAIL was but Gary said that it was like the CHAMPAGNE COCKTAILS the teachers loved except instead of champagne it had MANGO and PINEAPPLE.

So we all tasted our MOCKTAILS and they WERE delicious!

Maisie liked hers so much she didn't even really take a **BREATH**. She just kept sucking through the straw until it was all gone!

And that's when Gary said, "**OK**. Spill the beans, *compadres*. What's going on?"

And that's when Jodi said, "We think there might be something in the lake."

And **THAT'S** when I knew that Jodi had

NO INTENTION
OF TELLING

GARY THE

WHOLE STORY.

But then Gary said, "You mean the MONSTER. Go on."

And Jodi did a weird DOUBLE-BLINK THING and I knew that it was because she didn't realise that Gary knew about the MONSTER!

And that's when Jodi said, "We're on a mission to prove to the world that the monster exists. And we won't let anything or ANYONE get in the way. OK?"

And Zach said, "What?! Is that still the plan?! Even after it tried to EAT ME?!"

But then all of a sudden Miss Jones appeared. And she looked SHOCKED when she saw us all sitting in the hot tub with our swimming costumes on eating pizza and drinking MOCKTAILS.

And she said, "What on EARTH?! EVERYONE is waiting for you at the meeting point! We were supposed to be at the ROPE COURSE five minutes ago! Get out of there and let's go!"

Gary asked Miss Jones if she could pass him his robe and slippers, and Miss Jones did that thing that she does when she closes her eyes and breathes through her nose really

DEEPLY FOR AGES.

A Monster Ate My Packed Lunch!

When we got to the ROPE COURSE, I felt a bit sick. And that's when Zach said that he felt sick TOO and Miss Jones told us that you're not supposed to EAT in hot tubs because it can make you feel NAUSEOUS.

So I said that I didn't feel nauseous and

that I didn't even know what that WAS but that I just felt a bit like I was going to be SICK. But then Zach said that that was what feeling nauseous WAS.

I wasn't sure if I was feeling sick because of the

or the MONSTER TAIL or because the TREETOP ROPE COURSE was MUCH higher than I thought it was going to be. But it was probably because of ALL of them.

Ranger Tam asked who wanted to go up first, and before he had even finished his sentence, Jodi was standing RIGHT in front of him with her hand in the air.

But then Gary Petrie ran forward and said that HE wanted to go first and that's when Ranger Tam said that they could BOTH go first and Gary yelled,

"GP WINS AGAIN!"

(which didn't really make sense because they were both going first but that's just what

Gary's like sometimes).

We all watched as Jodi and Gary got their HELMETS and HARNESSES on and then Ranger Tam said, "OK, time to climb!"

That's when Jodi started to climb REALLY FAST and she was WAY AHEAD of Gary.

I thought she was doing it because she is MEGA COMPETITIVE (which means she likes to win at everything). But when she got to the very top she didn't go across the beam like she was supposed to. She just stood there STARING at something. And that's when I realised she was staring in the direction of the LAKE.

And then all of a sudden Jodi shouted down, "THE SHED BY THE LAKE. GO!"

I looked at Zach and Maisie and we all started to PANIC a bit because this was obviously about the MONSTER. And I knew that it meant Jodi had SPOTTED the monster near the shed and that she wanted us to go without her because she'd never get down in time.

I looked at Ranger Tam but he was too busy

trying to help Gary who'd got a bit stuck.

And then Jodi yelled,

"GO! GO! GO

NOW!"

So we ran.

When we got to the shed we saw that the

door was **WIDE OPEN**.

I could hardly **BREATHE** and it wasn't

just because we'd run **MEGA FAST**, it was

because I knew that there was SOMETHING inside it.

That's when we heard a noise coming from the shed and Zach turned and looked at me and I looked at him and then I tried to look at Maisie but that's when I realised that she wasn't there.

I looked down at the ground to see if she'd fainted but she wasn't there.

Then Zach said, "Over there. She's gone."

And I looked back the way we'd come and saw Maisie running back to the ROPE COURSE.

That's when I said, "It's just me and you.

Are you ready?"

And Zach gulped and nodded. And then he held up his phone to show he was ready to FILM the lake monster.

So we walked REALLY SLOWLY towards the shed and I put my finger to my lips to tell Zach to be COMPLETELY SILENT so that I could listen.

But to be honest, I had

how I was managing to be in CHARGE because I was

FREAKING OUT

on the inside! But Jodi wasn't there and this was SERIOUS so I knew that I had to be CALM and ORGANISED like she would be so that we didn't get eaten by the monster.

That's when we heard a SHUFFLING sound coming from inside the shed and Zach pointed to a small WINDOW at the top.

So I nodded and Zach lifted me up as much as he could and I pressed RECORD and lifted the phone up to the window.

But then we heard the shed door OPENING

and Zach put me down and we both lay
FLAT on the ground and didn't move, just
like Jodi had trained us to do.

And that's when we saw that it WASN'T
the lake monster leaving the shed – it was
the HOTEL OWNER.

So we waited until she was gone because
we obviously weren't supposed to be there
and we didn't want her to tell Miss Jones.

Then Zach said, "She came out of the shed.
We must have missed the monster and she
went in after it left."

And that's when I realised how LUCKY
she was and that if she had gone to the

shed probably even **ONE** minute before she would have come face to face with the

LAKE MONSTER.

That's when Zach said that we should look inside the shed for **EVIDENCE** that the monster had been there. So we got up and snuck round the side of the shed and tried the door but it was locked.

But then I remembered about the video so I said we could watch that and it might show us something since we couldn't get inside.

So I pressed play and that's when I

GASPED.

Zach said, "What is that? I can't tell. It's too shaky."

And the video WAS all shaky and blurry. But I still knew what we were looking at.

So I said, "Zach! That's the monster's TAIL!"

So we ran.

The Midnight Monster Tour

As SOON as we got back to the lodge Jodi wouldn't stop asking me and Zach the same questions OVER and OVER again. Like, were we SURE it was the monster's tail? And were we SURE we saw the hotel owner coming out of the shed?

And I was doing my best to stay calm and answer her questions but then there was a knock at the lodge door and I SCREAMED because I was

FREAKING OUT A BIT.

Jodi said that it was probably just Gary Petrie and that we should ignore it until she had finished the DEBRIEFING (which is what Jodi calls it when she has a lot of questions to ask someone about something

they've seen that she hasn't seen and it's very STRESSFUL).

But then a voice said, "Let me in, please. Right away."

And I looked at Jodi and she looked at me because it WASN'T Gary Petrie. It was Miss Jones!

And that's when Zach said, "I thought you covered for us!"

And Jodi said, "I did! I said that you felt sick after the hot-tub pizza and that you'd had to run back to your lodge to be sick and that Izzy had gone with you to make sure you were OK!"

Maisie jumped up and unlocked the door and let Miss Jones in.

And that's when we saw that she did **NOT** look happy!

Miss Jones walked over and sat down next to us and that's when Jodi slipped the

INVESTIGATION PAD

under the couch so Miss Jones wouldn't see it.

Then Miss Jones looked at Zach and said, "How are you feeling?"

And Zach **GULPED** and said that he was

feeling much better, thank you.

Then Miss Jones looked at me and that's when I remembered how SCARY Miss Jones could be when SHE thought that you'd done something WRONG.

And then she said, "Mrs Muir, the hotel owner, said she saw two pupils down by the lake at the store shed."

And that's when I could feel a WEIRD FEELING going through my FACE and my HANDS and then my LEGS.

But I stayed completely still and didn't say anything.

And then she looked at me and then at

Zach and then back to me and she said, "The two of you weren't in that shed, were you?"

And I shook my head and so did Zach, and I didn't feel too bad about doing it because it wasn't REALLY a lie because we HADN'T actually been INSIDE the shed.

And that's when Miss Jones said OK and that she needed to know where we were at ALL TIMES and we all nodded and she left.

And then as SOON as she had gone, Jodi said that the meeting had

OFFICIALLY

RESTARTED

and that we needed to keep a CLOSE EYE on MRS MUIR, the hotel owner.

So I asked Jodi what she meant and her EYES went WIDE and she said, "Are you being serious?!"

And that's when me and Zach both

GASPED

because we'd just realised that Mrs Muir had been in the shed at the SAME TIME as the monster!

I'd been so freaked out by seeing the BLURRY MONSTER TAIL in the video and knowing that it was IN THE SHED when we were standing RIGHT OUTSIDE that I hadn't even thought about Mrs Muir!

That's when Zach said, "I don't understand! Why didn't she scream?!"

And Jodi's eyes went WIDE and she said, "Because she KNEW it was in there. She KNOWS it. It might even be her PET!"

And Zach

GASPED AGAIN

and said, "You're right! AND I know what she's DOING! I know what she was doing in the shed! She's feeding it! It IS her pet!"

And then Zach got a really SERIOUS look on his face and said, "I think she's feeding it because it comes out of the lake when it's hungry and she doesn't want it to eat US!"

Later we ate our dinner as FAST as we could at the hotel and it wasn't just because MRS MUIR was there. It was because Jodi had said that we had to get BETTER FOOTAGE of the LAKE MONSTER and that we had to get it

TONIGHT

before it was

TOO LATE.

I knew what Jodi meant. She meant that we needed to get our EVIDENCE before the monster got so hungry that it ended up eating one of us!

But when Mrs Muir put our DESSERTS down on the table, Maisie SCREAMED and then Zach GASPED and Mrs Muir got a WEIRD LOOK on her face and then she put her hands behind her back REALLY FAST and walked away.

I had

NO IDEA

what the SCREAMING and GASPING had been about but then Zach looked at us and said, "Her HANDS. Did you see??"

And Maisie nodded and the table started shaking.

But me and Jodi shook our heads and then Jodi said, "I saw her hide them behind her back. Why did she do that? What did you see?"

And that's when Zach did a GULP and said, "They had green CRUSTY BITS on them. I think it's

DRIED MONSTER SLIME."

Once we got back to the lodge, Jodi said that we were going to be doing a STAKE-OUT, which is something that has NOTHING to

do with STEAK the food and is just a really PROFESSIONAL way of saying that we were going to be staying up ALL NIGHT LONG, looking out the Big Window until we spotted the LAKE MONSTER.

Jodi said that we had to keep ALL the lights turned OFF to do the

STAKE-OUT.

But Maisie started freaking out a bit because she has a PORTABLE NIGHT LIGHT that she takes with her when she stays over at places and she even takes it when she stays over Jodi's house and at my house and it keeps me awake because it's a bit too bright.

But then Jodi said that if the curtains were open wide and it was DARK outside and we had a light on INSIDE, then people and OTHER THINGS would be able to see inside. And that opening the curtains and turning off ALL the lights would make us INVISIBLE.

And that's when Maisie nodded and said that she didn't want her night light any more and that she would just hug her whale, FRANCISCO, instead.

So I said that I would do my STAKE-OUT SHIFT with Maisie and that we would go first.

I could TELL by the look on Jodi's face that she didn't want me and Maisie to go FIRST because she doesn't like not being involved and not controlling

EVERYTHING.

So she said that she would just sleep on the chair in the living room so she could be READY if needed. And Zach said that he would sleep on the couch.

So me and Maisie pulled all the cushions over to the window and made a STAKE-OUT DEN and it was quite fun to begin with, but after an hour it got a bit BORING because there was nothing to see outside except for the lake.

That's when Maisie said that we should phone ROOM SERVICE and get SNACKS like Gary had and that maybe Jonathan could bring us some MOCKTAILS.

I didn't think that Jodi would APPROVE of us getting mocktails when we were meant to be doing a

SERIOUS INVESTIGATION.

But then I looked over at the chair and saw that she was fast asleep and DROOLING a bit so I just said yes.

But we couldn't find the WELCOME PACK Gary had mentioned ANYWHERE so we didn't know what number to call.

That's when Maisie said, "I can text Gary. He'll be able to help us. He's got a mobile too."

I looked at Jodi again because I knew she would be FURIOUS if Gary found out about the

LAKE MONSTER STAKE-OUT.

But she was drooling even MORE now so I said, "OK. But don't tell him about the stake-out. And ask him to bring us packed lunches!"

Twenty minutes later I almost JUMPED out of my SKIN when a FIGURE appeared right in front of the Big Window!

But then I saw that the figure had a tray with two MOCKTAILS and two packed lunches and also that it was Gary Petrie.

Maisie waved at him but he didn't wave back and that's when I remembered what Jodi had said about it being like we were

INVISIBLE because all the lights were off.

So Maisie went RIGHT up to glass and shone the PHONE LIGHT on her face and Gary JUMPED and then laughed and put the packed lunches down and did the same. And then they BOTH pretended to be GHOSTS at each other through the glass.

And eventually Gary waved bye and ran off.

I couldn't WAIT to go and get the packed lunches because I was hoping there were loads of SANDWICHES in there, especially the BRIE ONES with GRAPES because I didn't think that I liked cheese like BRIE until I tried them at Gary's lodge and they were

AMAZING.

But Maisie made us wait for a while because she said she wanted to be

ONE HUNDRED
PER CENT SURE

that the LAKE MONSTER wasn't out there and that was a good point so we waited.

Then, when we were sure, we snuck over to the front door and unlocked it really quietly and slipped out.

But as SOON as we got outside, we heard NOISES at the lake.

Maisie grabbed my hand and tried to pull me back inside but I stayed still and listened because I wanted to make sure that it wasn't just someone walking past or a bird or something because I REALLY wanted my packed lunch!

But then we heard SPLASHING and

weird SLUDGING SOUNDS like someone or SOMETHING was walking in wet mud. And then there was a weird SLURPING SOUND and that's when I looked at Maisie and hissed, "Open the door. NOW!"

Maisie unlocked the door and we LEAPED inside and locked it behind us with a loud THUD.

That's when Jodi jumped up and said, "WHAT? WHERE? I'M READY!"

And Zach groaned and rolled off the couch and landed on the floor.

Then Maisie RAN over to the window and just stood there and didn't say anything.

So I went over to see if she was OK and that's when I saw that she had her eyes SHUT TIGHT.

But I knew that she was OK because she was pointing the phone at the window and it was recording!

I looked out the window but I couldn't see anything, just the lake. And that's when Jodi came over and asked what was going on so I explained about the SPLASHING and the SLUDGING and the SLURPING noises that we'd heard when we went outside to get the sandwiches.

Jodi looked SHOCKED and she said,

"What packed lunch?!"

And I didn't have time to explain so I just pointed out the window and said, "Those o—"

But I couldn't finish my sentence because the food Gary had left us was GONE.

And that's when I looked at Zach and said, "You were right. It IS coming out of the water because it's hungry. The monster ate our

PACKED LUNCHES!"

Jodi made us all watch the film on Zach's phone over and over again but none of us could see the MONSTER.

Zach said that what we'd heard must have been the monster coming out of the lake and walking towards the lodge because it had smelled the

PACKED LUNCHES.

and that by the time we had got back inside and started filming it had devoured the FEAST and slipped back into the lake. And Jodi said that that made sense because she thought Jonathan's sandwiches smelled delicious, especially the ones with

CHEESE and PICKLE.

And then Jodi got a weird look on her face and for a second I thought that it was because the

MONSTER

was back! But then I realised that she was

just thinking about sandwiches.

But then all of a sudden we heard **SPLASHING** and Jodi

RAN out of the cabin.

So we all ran after her and when we got outside we found her standing next to the lake taking **PHOTOS** of the ground.

And then she turned to us and said, "It must have still been here but it's gone now. Look!"

Maisie **GRABBED** my hand and squeezed it tight and we walked over to Jodi.

Jodi took something out of her

SURVIVAL SUIT

and got down on the ground and that's when I saw that it was a MEASURING TAPE and that she was measuring a giant FOOTPRINT.

Then all of a sudden there was MORE SPLASHING in the lake a few metres away and we all FROZE and held our breath.

And then we heard SNORTING.

I was just about to say that we should GET OUT OF HERE ASAP when Maisie

GASPED and said,

"OH NO!
PLEASE, NO!"

And I looked at her and she had gone
REALLY PALE. And she was pointing
at something next to the water and we all
looked and saw that it was a WHITE ROBE.

And that's when Maisie looked up at us
with BIG EYES and said, "That's GARY'S
ROBE."

And I GASPED because I realised that
Gary must never have made it back to his
lodge after he'd brought us the sandwiches.

The lake monster had

☆ GOT HIM! ☆

Where's Gary?

Maisie GRABBED the phone out of Jodi's hand and called Gary Petrie's number. Then her eyes went WIDE and she said, "Hello? GARY?!"

Then she took the phone away from her ear and her eyes were ENORMOUS.

And Jodi said, "What happened? Did he answer??"

And that's when Maisie said that someone or **SOMETHING** had answered but she could only hear **SPLASHING SOUNDS**.

Then Maisie got a really

SERIOUS

look on her face and said, "There might still be hope. He might have managed to get away. Let's go!"

And then she started running along the side of the lake.

But we all just stood there because we had **NO IDEA** what was going on or where Maisie wanted us to go.

"Where are you **GOING**?!" shouted Jodi.

And Maisie stopped and turned round and said, "We need to get out on the lake and try to save Gary! It's almost midnight! Ranger Tam's tour is about to leave. Let's **GO**!"

When we arrived at the dock there were **LOADS** of people waiting to get on the boat.

Jodi hissed, "Now's our chance. Follow me and **STAY DOWN**."

So we all followed her and she rushed to join the back of the queue JUST as the last people were stepping on board.

And then she stepped on to the boat and said, "Grab a life jacket and meet me BELOW DECK."

Then she took one of the life jackets and put it on and started CRAWLING along the deck.

So we did the same and once we got

BELOW DECK Jodi made us all hide under a big BLANKET she'd found and stay COMPLETELY STILL. So we did.

And that's when we heard the boat start to MOVE and I got a bit excited because even though this was SERIOUSLY SCARY I'd never really been on a boat like this one before, especially not at midnight!

Jodi said that we needed to be EXTRA CAREFUL while we were ON BOARD and

that boats were **NO JOKE** and that this was **SERIOUS** and also **DANGEROUS**, because of the water, and we all nodded loads.

Jodi said that the rule was to stay in **PAIRS** at **ALL** times. And not to **RUN**. Not even if we saw the

MONSTER

and we all agreed. Then she said that once we went **ON DECK** we had to hide behind the other passengers so that Ranger Tam didn't see us or we'd get in trouble because we didn't have permission to be here and also because we hadn't bought TICKETS.

That's when Zach said that people who did what we had done were called STOWAWAYS and that we might get put in

JAIL.

And that's when Maisie took a DEEP BREATH and said that THAT was a risk she was willing to take to save GARY'S LIFE and that if they wanted to put her in jail for that they could.

Jodi said, "Me too!"

Then me and Zach said it too because everyone else was saying it and also because we knew it was the RIGHT THING to do.

Then Jodi said that the plan was to search the LAKE with our EYES while we were ON DECK to see if we could spot Gary trying to swim away from the monster or holding on to a ROCK waiting to be rescued or anything.

And then Jodi gave me a bit of a SIDE LOOK and I knew she was scared that we WOULDN'T find Gary because he'd already been EATEN.

Jodi checked that we all had our LIFE

JACKETS on properly because she was
worried and also because she likes to check

EVERYTHING

because she doesn't really trust other people
to do things properly.

When it was time to go up ON DECK, Jodi
smiled at me a TINY BIT when no one was
looking and I knew that it was because she
was enjoying the mission, too (even though it
was a very serious and DANGEROUS one).

But then all of a sudden there was loads of NOISE on deck and people were

GASPING

and moving around a LOT.

That's when Jodi looked at us and said, "This is IT, people. Stay together. DON'T run. Let's GO!"

So we all followed Jodi up the stairs on to the deck and that's when we saw that EVERYONE was

STARING

at something in the distance and Ranger Tam was SHINING A LIGHT on to the water and shouting, "WOW! Did everyone see that?! I can't BELIEVE IT! I think this is the very FIRST sighting of her HEAD!"

That's when we all looked out on to the lake.

And Jodi

And I held on TIGHT to Maisie in case she fainted.

I couldn't BELIEVE what we were SEEING

because what we were seeing was a

MONSTER HEAD

bobbing around in the lake!

And because of the spotlight we could even see its big black EYES!

Then suddenly a voice behind us said, "Did you see it?! It's the

And we GASPED and spun around because it was GARY PETRIE!

Maisie GRABBED him and hugged him for ages and he smiled LOADS. And then she asked him what he was doing on the boat and he said that he'd sneaked on just like us because he wanted to see

THE MONSTER.

Then JODI grabbed him and gave him a quick hug too and he looked SHOCKED.

And that's when he said, "OK. What's going on?"

And that's when Jodi said, "No time to explain. Zach! Pass me the phone!"

But Zach just smiled because he was already RECORDING.

And Jodi said, "We're going to be

FAMOUS!"

Then she made us hide under the blanket until every single passenger was off the boat and it had gone quiet.

And then we crept off the boat and on to

the dock. But that's when we heard a voice say, "I think you owe me TICKET MONEY, don't you?"

And we all GASPED and turned around and that's when we saw Ranger Tam was still on the boat and he was standing with his arms crossed, STARING at us!

I didn't know if we should say something or try to give him some money or if we should just RUN. But before we could do anything he said, "Did you think I wouldn't notice you'd snuck on to my boat? I knew you were there. But I saw you all had life jackets on and were following the rules so I didn't say anything. Just kept an eye on you. Didn't want to have to take you back and give everyone a refund, did I? Tonight was a BIG NIGHT for us!"

And then he smiled a bit of a CREEPY SMILE and said, "Now off to bed with the lot of you before the

LAKE MONSTER

gets you!"

So we RAN back to the lodges.

But when we got there, Gary said, "LOOK! A giant footprint!"

And we said that we already knew about
that and that it belonged to the **MONSTER**.

And then Gary said, "Where do they lead?"

And Jodi's head spun **RIGHT** round to
face Gary when he said that and then she
said, "What do you mean?"

And Gary pointed to the ground and said,
"There's loads of them, look. They must go
somewhere!"

And that's when I **GASPED** and said that
the monster must have come **BACK**, looking
for **MORE PACKED LUNCHES**.

And that's when **GARY** gasped too and
he said, "Why did you feed it my packed

lunches?!"

And he looked a bit annoyed with me.

But I didn't have time to explain because Jodi said we needed to follow the footprints NOW before the monster found SOMEONE to eat!

Jodi ran ahead of us but then all of a sudden she STOPPED.

And Zach hissed, "What? What is it?"

We all watched as Jodi turned around REALLY SLOWLY and her face looked

MEGA WEIRD.

And that's when she said, "We've got a problem.

A **BIG** PROBLEM."

And she was **RIGHT** because the footsteps led all the way to the

BOYS' LODGE.

That's when Gary RUSHED past us and went round the back of the lodge and we heard him SCREAM.

So we all ran after him and I was ONE HUNDRED PER CENT expecting to see the

LAKE MONSTER.

But we didn't.

That's when Gary said, "It's RUINED. Look at it!"

We saw that he was screaming about his HOT-TUB because it was COVERED in MUD and the water was all BROWN.

Then Gary turned and looked at us and said, "Why would the monster do this to my hot-tub?"

And he looked like he was going to cry.

That's when Zach GASPED and said that he thought the lake monster could probably only stay out of the water for so long before it needed to make itself WET again. And that it was probably TOO DRY by the time it got to the lodges so it had to use the HOT-TUB to get all SLIMY again.

And that's when Gary fell to his KNEES and said that he was GUTTED about the hot tub and that he'd wanted to use it at LEAST five more times before we left.

Jodi said that Gary needed to FORGET

about the hot tub and get his HEAD
STRAIGHT and that there was probably a
LAKE MONSTER inside the lodge

EATING EVERYONE.

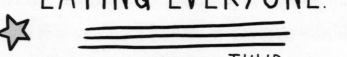

And that's when I heard a THUD and I saw
that Maisie had fainted. And to be honest
I was a bit surprised that it had taken her
THIS long because Jodi had talked about
the monster eating people at LEAST three
times that night.

That's when Jodi said that she was

GOING IN.

But then Gary said, "I'm going in first because it's MY lodge."

And for once Jodi didn't argue.

Gary got a bit of a LOOK on his face and then he said, "Right. Um. OK. Let's go then."

And I knew that it was because he had expected Jodi to say NO and that now he was shocked that HE had to go first when there was probably a

Jodi took a deep breath and said to me and Zach, "Stay with Maisie. And if we're not back in exactly FOUR MINUTES, call the ARMY. OK?"

So we nodded and then we watched as they disappeared inside the lodge. And then we stood in SILENCE for

FOUR FULL MINUTES.

And I knew that it was four minutes because Zach had set the STOP WATCH on his phone and he was holding it out in front of us so we could both see.

I was JUST about to say that we needed to phone the ARMY when both Jodi and Gary came RUSHING out of the cabin and Jodi hissed, "Mr Beattie's GONE!"

I looked at Zach and Zach looked at me and I knew that we were both thinking the same thing. The lake monster had TAKEN MR BEATTIE.

So I said, "Are you sure?"

Jodi nodded and said that his bedroom door had been WIDE OPEN and that there was mud

ALL OVER THE FLOOR.

And that's when I gasped because that was PROOF that the monster had taken him!

Then Jodi said, "We need to get back down to the lake. They might still be there!"

And then Gary shouted,

"WAIT!

I'VE GOT AN IDEA!"

And then he ran back inside the lodge and came back a few seconds later with two cans of DEODORANT.

And then he said, "If the monster's with Mr Beattie, I'm going to SPRAY IT with THESE so it goes all DRY and CRUSTY and has to run back to the lake! That'll teach it to use MY hot tub!"

I looked at Jodi and she looked IMPRESSED and I was a bit impressed TOO because it was a good idea!

And then Jodi said,

Me and Zach each picked Maisie up by an arm and a leg and Gary Petrie ran ahead with a deodorant can in each hand, waving his arms in the air and shouting, "WE'RE COMING, MR BEATTIE! HANG ON!"

But when we got to the lake there was no one there.

Jodi said we should look around a bit so we did, and that's when I found Gary's robe where we'd left it by our lodge. So I walked over and handed it to Gary.

And Gary gave me a weird look and said, "What's that?"

I was a bit surprised when he said that because we all knew how much he LOVED his robe.

So I said, "It's your ROBE. We found it here earlier, right next to the lake. That's why we went on the tour. We thought you'd been attacked by the monster after you'd delivered our sandwiches."

Gary looked

MEGA CONFUSED.

And then he unzipped his WATERPROOF JACKET and we all saw that he was WEARING his robe underneath!

Then Gary took the robe from me and held it out in front of him and said,

"This is MASSIVE."

Then he

GASPED

and said,

"It's an XXL!

It's an ADULT robe!"

And then Gary looked at the ground and said, "We're too late. Poor Mr Beattie. He wasn't even that old!"

Warm Shoes

None of us knew what you should do when your teacher gets eaten by a monster.

Zach said that he thought it was time to call the **ARMY** so that they could come and **CAPTURE** the monster before it ate any more teachers.

Maisie said that it was time to GO HOME and that we needed to go and tell Miss Jones

EVERYTHING.

But then Jodi got a bit ANGRY and she said, "Someone has to stop her."

And I thought Jodi meant the MONSTER.

But then she said, "I'm going to tell Mrs Muir that her PET has EATEN our teacher and that SHE should have called the army AGES ago rather than keeping a DANGEROUS ANIMAL in a LAKE!"

And Jodi looked absolutely FURIOUS

and I knew that there was no point trying to argue with her so we all just ran after her, and Gary said that he was going to bring the ROBE as EVIDENCE.

We all followed Jodi up the steps and into the RECEPTION and watched as she marched RIGHT up to the desk and pressed the bell really hard THREE TIMES and then crossed her arms and waited. But no one came.

And that's when Zach said, "The shed."

We all looked at each other because we knew that he was RIGHT and that that's where the hotel owner would be. But also that the MONSTER might be there, too.

That's when Maisie took a really deep breath and said, "We need to do this, people."

And I almost laughed because she sounded EXACTLY like Jodi and I knew that she was being

MEGA BRAVE.

So that's when we all looked at each other.

And then Jodi nodded.

So we RAN.

When we got to the shed, the door was closed.

That's when Gary Petrie said, "What now? Do we knock?"

We all looked at each other but no one said anything and I knew that it was because no one wanted to be the one who knocked in case the **MONSTER** opened the door!

And then all of a sudden Jodi stepped forward and pushed the door

WIDE OPEN.

But the shed was empty.

That's when Jodi said, "Get inside. Quick!"

So we all RAN inside and Jodi shut the door behind us and my heart was RACING because I thought she'd seen the monster or something!

But then she said, "We need to search quick before Miss Muir finds us here. There might be evidence we can use to prove she's keeping a pet monster."

So we looked around the shed but there wasn't much there except for some beach equipment and loads of towels.

But Zach said, "That's weird."

And we all looked at him and saw that he was pointing at clothes hanging on the back of the shed door. And then he took something down from a hook and held it up and we all saw that it was a woman's shirt and that it had a NAME TAG on it and that the name tag said MARGARET MUIR.

And Zach pointed at a pair of SHOES on the ground and then he bent down and put his HAND inside one of them and Gary Petrie yelled,

"YUCK!"

I knew that the clothes and shoes were obviously Mrs Muir's but I didn't understand why Zach looked so freaked out or why he was putting his hands inside them!

That's when Zach said, "Why would she leave her clothes in here?"

And Gary said that maybe this was where she got changed for work. But Zach said that didn't make any sense because it wasn't anywhere near the hotel and it was right by the lake.

And then he said, "I think she was here a second ago and she left her clothes behind. Her shoes are still warm."

And Gary Petrie made a

SICK SOUND

and I knew that it was because of the WARM SHOES.

We all STARED at each other because this didn't make ANY sense.

But then Zach said, "Do you remember Mrs Muir's hands? How green and a bit scaly they looked? And how she hid them from us?"

That's when Jodi said that the green stuff was from the

LAKE MONSTER

because she'd been feeding it and maybe even stroking it, too.

But Zach shook his head and said, "I think

we've got this all wrong."

And then he looked up at us and his eyes were HUGE and his face had gone completely WHITE.

And then he said, "I don't think Mrs Muir KNOWS the monster. I think she IS the monster!"

We all GASPED and stared at Zach with

WIDE EYES.

Then Zach said that Jodi must have seen

Mrs Muir go into the shed in

MONSTER FORM

that time and that me and Zach had seen

her come out in

HUMAN WOMAN FORM!

That's when Gary looked at Jodi and did a bit of a NERVOUS LAUGH and said, "I bet you're glad you didn't give her a piece of your mind now! She probably would have eaten you!"

And then Jodi gulped and I said, "I think that's why she UPGRADED us. She wanted us all to be close to the lake so she could EAT US!"

And that's when Maisie screamed, "THE LODGES! COME ON! WE NEED TO SAVE MISS JONES AND EVERYONE ELSE!"

And then she ran out of the shed and we

all ran after her.

But when we got to the lake, we heard **SPLASHING** and Gary shouted, "You can come out, Mrs Muir. We know it's you in there! We're not scared of you!"

And we all **GASPED** because we were actually **VERY SCARED** and we knew that it was a

to ask **A MONSTER** to come ashore in case it **ATE US!**

Then the splashing got **LOUDER** and we

heard **SNORTING TOO!**

I had no idea what was going on but then Maisie said, "That sounds like Miss Jones! She snorts like that sometimes when she laughs. Maybe she does it when she's scared, too!"

And that's when Jodi took out her torch and pointed it at the lake and we saw that **ALL** the teachers were in the lake!

Then Gary said, "Oh no! They're having a midnight swim! And they have

NO IDEA

THERE'S A

TEACHER-EATING

MONSTER

in there!"

That's when we started to

PANIC!

So we all began jumping up and down and waving our arms about to try to get their attention and Jodi yelled, "TEACHERS! Can you hear us?"

But it was obvious that they COULDN'T because they were all laughing too loudly and splashing about.

That's when Maisie started blowing her EMERGENCY WHISTLE that her mum makes her wear after the time we went on the school trip with the WEREWOLF.

And Gary yelled,

"GET OUT OF THERE
BEFORE YOU
GET EATEN
LIKE MR BEATTIE!"

Then all of a sudden, Ranger Tam appeared and he said, "What on EARTH do you think you're doing? There are guests trying to sleep! Stop yelling!"

But then we heard an

ENORMOUS
SPLASHING
SOUND

and we saw a TAIL in the lake just a few metres away from where the teachers were having their midnight swim!

That's when Gary told Zach to start filming

because that's what Mr Beattie would have wanted.

And then Maisie screamed at the top of her lungs,

"SWIM FOR YOUR LIVES!!!

IT'S THE LAKE MONSTER! AND IT EATS TEACHERS!"

But before anyone could do ANYTHING, the monster swam RIGHT past the teachers! They all started SCREAMING and SHOUTING and trying to run out of the water.

We all stood and watched in

SHOCK

as the monster swam CLOSER and CLOSER to the shore and then it walked RIGHT OUT OF THE WATER and stood in front of us!

It Came From Out of the Lake

The monster **STARED** at Zach, who was still holding out his phone even though his hand was **REALLY SHAKING**.

The monster didn't move. It just stayed completely **STILL**.

I had to take **DEEP BREATHS** because I

couldn't believe how

WEIRD

and

SLIMY it looked

and how LONG

and

SPIKY its tail was

or how **BUMPY** and

SCARY its head was!

That's when Jodi said, "Hello, Mrs Muir. Don't you look nice this evening? We'd like to ask you a few questions if that's OK? About our teacher, Mr Beattie?"

And I GULPED because I thought we were all about to witness Jodi being eaten ALIVE.

But then all of a sudden, the monster raised its SLIMY ARMS in the air and started to

PULL ITS HEAD OFF.

And that's when I felt Maisie's hand go **LIMP** in mine and then she hit the ground with a little thud.

And when I looked back up at the monster I couldn't **BELIEVE** what I was seeing because I was looking at a

MONSTER

with a

HUMAN HEAD.

Then the monster dropped its head on the ground and it rolled over towards us and we all GASPED.

It took me AGES to realise what I was looking at. And we were all in

SHOCK

because the

LAKE MONSTER

was actually

MRS MUIR in a

MONSTER COSTUME.

We all **STARED** at her and no one said anything for **AGES** until Zach eventually said, "Why are you pretending to be a monster? Why are you trying to trick everyone?"

And that's when Mrs Muir opened her mouth. But nothing came out so she shut it again.

And then Ranger Tam stepped forward and said, "Look. It's just a bit of fun. We needed to make money to keep this place going, all right? And it was going really well until you kids came along!"

And Mrs Muir said, "It's OK, Tam. Thanks for sticking up for me. You're a great ranger."

And that's when Mrs Muir did a really long sigh and then she said, "It all started a year ago. Business wasn't as good as it used to be and the place was looking a bit outdated. People want FANCY RESORTS with SPAS and HOT TUBS these days so we were losing business. If it wasn't for the school visits, we would have had to shut down years ago! So we always try to make sure the schools have a good time and keep coming back."

And then she looked at Miss Jones and gave her a little smile and I realised that that was why we'd been given the UPGRADE and all the extra stuff because they wanted us to come back again next year.

Then Mrs Muir said, "So we decided to update the place and build these luxury lakeside lodges. And it was going well for the first few months until a very fancy spa retreat opened up the road and everyone started going there instead. We were running out of money. At one point I thought the electricity company were going to switch our electricity off!"

And that's when I realised that that was why Ranger Tam had looked so worried when the lights went out the other night at dinner.

Then Mrs Muir took a deep breath and said, "That's when I decided to use the Legend of the Lake to attract visitors. And it worked! That and offering lots of extras to our guests. Jonathan has even been cooking cheeseburgers at MIDNIGHT if the pupils request it!"

And that's when Miss Jones looked at ME
but I shook my head

LOADS.

And then she looked at Gary and he just
sort of looked down at the ground and Miss
Jones rolled her eyes.

Mrs Muir sat down on the ground and her
big tail

SWOOSHED

the grass.

And that's when Jodi looked at Ranger Tam and said, "That's why you got us off the lake so fast when we were doing raft building. You didn't want us to realise the tail was a

FAKE."

Ranger Tam put his head down and nodded and said that Mrs Muir had lost it the night before and that it wasn't CHEAP and that he needed us away from the lake so he could go in and fish it out.

Then Jodi said to Mrs Muir, "So it WAS you I saw going into the shed when I was on

the ropes course. Why were you dressed as the monster during the day?"

And Mrs Muir sighed and said, "We had a lot of tourists out on the water that day so I went out swimming so there'd be a few 'sightings'."

Then Zach said, "How do you swim with that costume on? It's huge!"

And that's when Mrs Muir explained that it was actually very

LIGHTWEIGHT

and that she had been a champion swimmer

when she was young so she found it easy to
swim underwater wearing it.

And Zach said, "Cool!"

And that made Mrs Muir smile a bit.

Then she said, "I really am sorry if we've
upset or frightened anyone. That wasn't our

intention. We wanted everyone to have a great, exciting time here and to come back. But I understand that we've tricked people and that isn't right. I'm sorry."

And then she looked at Miss Jones and said, "If you would like a refund we can arrange that. I understand."

But Miss Jones said that wouldn't be necessary and that we'd all had a lovely time and that made Mrs Muir smile again.

And that's when GARY stepped forward and said, "But what about

THIS?!"

And then he held up Mr Beattie's ROBE
and said, "We found it down by the water.
Mr Beattie is

MISSING!"

But a voice from the back of the crowd
said, "I'm not missing!"

And we all turned round and saw Mr
Beattie!

So that's when we said that we'd found his
robe by the lake and asked why he hadn't

been in bed and why there had been mud

ALL OVER

HIS BEDROOM.

And then Gary said, "We thought the lake

monster had

 EATEN YOU!"

 And Mr Beattie looked a bit

EMBARRASSED.

And then he said, "Um. We all fancied a night swim in the lake. But then I needed to use the bathroom and I couldn't remember where I'd left my robe. It was dark and muddy and I didn't have a torch. I was stumbling around the lodges for ages trying to find my way but I had mud in my EYES."

And then Gary Petrie

GASPED and said,

"It was YOU who made my hot tub all muddy!"

And Mr Beattie said, "I was trying to get

some of the mud off me before I went into the lodge. I was COVERED IN IT."

And that's when I

GASPED and said,

"You didn't see any packed lunches on your way, did you?!"

And Mr Beattie's face went RED and he said, "I thought someone had ordered room service and forgot about it because it was so late. So I took them back to the lodge with me for, um, safekeeping."

And then he looked even MORE

embarrassed because we all knew that he'd stolen the sandwiches and eaten them in Gary's HOT TUB.

And then Miss Jones looked at us and said, "What were you all doing out of your lodges and down near the lake ANYWAY?!"

And we all

STARED

at each other because we knew that we were in

Ranger Tam laughed really loud and said "You were investigating, weren't you? You knew something wasn't right. You'll make fine rangers one day!"

And we all nodded loads. But Miss Jones carried on looking at us for a long time and I knew that we were still in

Then Zach said, "Is that why the lake is called MENTORS LAKE?"

And Mrs Muir looked puzzled.

So Zach said, "MENTORS is an anagram

of MONSTER."

And Mrs Muir

GASPED

and said that she'd never realised that before! And that it had been called Mentors Lake for ever. And that the

MONSTER SIGHTINGS

had been going on for over

ONE HUNDRED YEARS.

And then all of a sudden there was a

HUGE SPLASH

from the middle of

the lake and everyone

GASPED!

But when Jodi and Ranger Tam shone their
torches on the lake there was nothing there.
And that's when we all STARED at each
other and Zach GULPED because we knew

there was a

REAL

monster out there somewhere.

And it was

WATCHING

US

Acknowledgements

Love, hugs and a great big THANK YOU to my
brilliant editor, Kirsty Stansfield (Gary Petrie 4EVA!).

TOM! I am the luckiest author ever to be able to work
with you on the Izzy books. Thank you so much for all
your hard work. Massive thanks to super-designer,
Nicola also. This book DEFINITELY has some
of the FUNNIEST illustrations so far!
(The Gary Petrie illos are a TRIUMPH.)

Huge thanks to my awesome agent, Becky.
I'm so thankful for all that you do to support me.
You're amazing. More hugs and thanks to Rebecca, Fi,
Halimah and everyone at Nosy Crow who worked
on the book. You all ROCK.

Most of all, thank you to my wonderful wee boy, Albie.
You inspire me every day. I can't wait to have more beach
and lake adventures with you. I love you.

Another hilarious
adventure with Izzy
and friends!

THE
BROKEN
LEG OF
DOOM

Read on for a
SNEAK PEEK!

Bad Things Always Happen in Threes

I **KNEW** something bad was going to happen as **SOON** as we arrived at the hospital.

And I knew it because my mum says that bad things always happen in **THREES**. And **TWO** bad things had already happened that day because Jodi made us all do **EXTREME**

DANCING (which is when you dance as FAST as you can for as LONG as you can) and Maisie had got dizzy and fallen and broken her LEG. And then when we were in Jodi's mum's car following the ambulance to the hospital, I reached into my bag to get my **TWIX** because I was **STARVING** after all the dancing but it was **GONE**. And that's when I remembered that I'd already eaten it on my way to school.

So anyway, when we got to the hospital, I got a **WEIRD FEELING**. And it was because of the **CREEPY STATUE** in the entrance. And the **WEIRD SHAPE** of Maisie's **LEG** under the blanket. And the **STRANGE BOY** with the **FEATHER** in his hat.

But it was when we found out about the **CURSE** that we **KNEW**.

Maisie and her LEG were in

DEEP
TROUBLE.

Dancing Injury to the Right Leg

When we arrived at the hospital Jodi's mum parked the car and Zach yelled, "There's the ambulance. Look!" So I looked and that's when I saw the ambulance doors BURST open and Jodi came rushing out, pulling Maisie's stretcher behind her.

Jodi had REFUSED to come with us in the car to the hospital because she said she needed to stay with Maisie. And the paramedics had let her because Jodi told them she was Maisie's GUARDIAN because Maisie's mum wasn't there yet and that Maisie NEEDED HER and also that she would CHAIN herself to Maisie's stretcher IF NEED BE.

So me and Zach and Jodi's mum RAN after Maisie's stretcher into the

ACCIDENT AND EMERGENCY

bit of the hospital and up to the reception desk.

And before the paramedics could even say ONE WORD Jodi shouted,

"FEMALE.
AGED EIGHT YEARS,
FIVE AND A HALF MONTHS.
DANCING INJURY TO
THE RIGHT LEG.
POTENTIALLY BROKEN
IN NUMEROUS PLACES."

And as SOON as Jodi said that, Maisie SCREAMED at the top of her LUNGS and

everyone in the waiting room GASPED and the receptionist covered her ears with her hands because Maisie's scream is MEGA LOUD.

That's when one of the doctors came running over to see what was wrong. But then all of a sudden Maisie stopped screaming MID-SCREAM and closed her eyes and went COMPLETELY STILL.

So that's when I explained that Maisie had FAINTED from SHOCK because of what Jodi had just said and that it happened all the time. And that she'd wake up in a minute and need a Ribena and probably a Twix too,

and that I had some Ribena but that I didn't have a Twix. And then I explained about the TWIX THING and bad things happening in THREES.

But the doctor just stood there with a PANICKED look on his face and I started to worry because he didn't look that much older than my cousin Toby and he's still at secondary school. But then I noticed that he was wearing a hoody and carrying a bunch of grapes and that he was a visitor. And that he'd probably just come running over because of the noise Maisie was making.

Then Jodi started shouting for a

STETHOSCOPE so she could check Maisie's

VITAL ORGANS.

And a nurse appeared and said that she was going to take Maisie behind a little curtain to do an EXAMINATION and that we should all wait in the WAITING AREA, especially Jodi. And then she gave Jodi a bit of a LOOK so we went.